MAGAZINE

Tin House

Volume 16, Number 4

*"In the depth of winter I finally learned that
there was in me an invincible summer."*

—ALBERT CAMUS

TROMPE L'OEIL

a novel by Nancy Reisman

During a vacation in Rome, the Murphy family experiences a life-altering tragedy. In the immediate aftermath, James, Nora, and their children find solace in their Massachusetts coast home, but as the years pass the weight of the loss disintegrates the increasingly fragile marriage and leaves its mark on each family member. *Trompe l'Oeil* seamlessly alternates among several characters' points of view, capturing the details of their daily lives as well as their longing for connection and fear of abandonment. Through the turbulence of marriage, the challenges of parenthood, job upheavals, and calamities large and small, *Trompe l'Oeil* examines family legacies, the ways those legacies persist, and the ways they might be transcended.

"This a beautiful and deeply satisfying novel."

—MARGOT LIVESEY, author of
The Flight of Gemma Hardy

Available May 2015

WONDERING WHO YOU ARE

a memoir by Sonya Lea

In the twenty-third year of their marriage, Sonya Lea's husband, Richard, went in for surgery to treat a rare cancer. When he came out, he had no recollection of their life together: how they met, their wedding day, the births of their two children. All of it was gone, along with the rockier parts of their past—her drinking, his anger. Richard could now hardly speak, emote, or make memories from moment to moment. Who he'd been, no longer was. *Wondering Who You Are* braids the story of Sonya and Richard's relationship, those memories that he could no longer conjure, with those fateful days in the hospital. As they build a fresh life together, as Richard develops a new personality, Sonya is forced to question her own assumptions and desires, her place in the marriage and her way of being in the world.

"*Wondering Who Your Are* is an amazing accomplishment. Every page sparkles with wisdom, candor, insight, and love."

—CHRISTOPHER RYAN, author of *Sex at Dawn*

Available July 2015

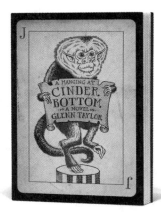

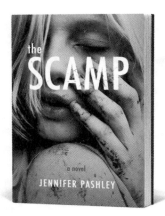

A HANGING AT CINDER BOTTOM

a novel by Glenn Taylor

The year is 1910. Halley's Comet has just signaled the end of the world, and Jack Johnson has knocked out the "Great White Hope," Jim Jeffries. On a rainy Sunday morning in August, the townspeople of Keystone, West Virginia are gathered in a red-light district known as Cinder Bottom to witness the public hanging of Abe Baach and Goldie Toothman. He's Keystone's most famous poker player who split town seven years prior under suspicion of murder; she's the madam of its most infamous brothel. When Abe returns to Keystone to reunite with Goldie and to set the past right, he finds a brother dead and his father's saloon in shambles. Only then, in facing his family's past, does the real swindle begin.

"Glenn Taylor's new novel defies classification or clichés. . . . It will clean your clock, fix your wagon, and knock you out."

—SUSAN STRAIGHT,
author of *Between Heaven and Here*

Available July 2015

THE SCAMP

a novel by Jennifer Pashley

Rayelle Reed can't escape in her small town, where everyone knows everything and not enough: All the guys she slept with, but not the ones she loved. The baby she had out of wedlock with the pastor's son, and how the baby died, but not the grief and guilt that consume her. Rayelle meets Couper Gale, a freelance detective on a mission to investigate a rash of missing girls, and she tags along as an excuse to cross the state line. But when Couper's investigation leads them to the mystery surrounding Rayelle's runaway cousin, Khaki, she finds she is heading straight back into everything she was hoping to leave behind.

"Gritty, seductive, and completely mesmerizing. . . . Be warned: these characters bloom so large on the page, you'll ignore the real world around you until the last tangled secret has been unraveled."

—SHANNA MAHIN,
author of *Oh! You Pretty Things*

Available August 2015

Tin House
MAGAZINE

EDITOR IN CHIEF / PUBLISHER
Win McCormack

EDITOR Rob Spillman
ART DIRECTOR Diane Chonette
MANAGING EDITOR Cheston Knapp
EXECUTIVE EDITOR Michelle Wildgen
POETRY EDITOR Matthew Dickman
EDITOR-AT-LARGE Elissa Schappell
POETRY EDITOR-AT-LARGE Brenda Shaughnessy
PARIS EDITOR Heather Hartley
ASSISTANT EDITORS Lance Cleland, Emma Komlos-Hrobsky
EDITORIAL ASSISTANT Thomas Ross

CONTRIBUTING EDITORS: Dorothy Allison, Steve Almond, Aimee Bender, Charles D'Ambrosio, Brian DeLeeuw, Anthony Doerr, CJ Evans, Nick Flynn, Matthea Harvey, Jeanne McCulloch, Christopher Merrill, Rick Moody, Whitney Otto, D. A. Powell, Jon Raymond, Rachel Resnick, Helen Schulman, Jim Shepard, Karen Shepard, Bill Wadsworth

DESIGNER: Jakob Vala

INTERNS: Talal Achi, Claire Gordon, Colin Houghton, Jess Kibler, Nell Pierce, Lauren Roberts, Kathryn Wilhelm

READERS: Stephanie Booth, Ansley Clark, Sarah Currin-Moles, Susan DeFreitas, Molly Dickinson, Polly Dugan, Megan Freshley, Selin Gokcesu, Todd Gray, Lisa Grgas, Dahlia Grossman-Heinze, Matthew Hall, Carol Keeley, Shayla Lawson, Louise Wareham Leonard, Julian Lucas, Curtis Moore, Ian Nelson, Sean Quinn, Gordon Smith, Jennifer Taylor, JR Toriseva, Lacy Warner

DEPUTY PUBLISHER Holly MacArthur
CIRCULATION DIRECTOR Laura Howard
DIRECTOR OF PUBLICITY Nanci McCloskey
COMPTROLLER Janice Carter

Tin House Books

EDITORIAL ADVISOR Rob Spillman
EDITORS Meg Storey, Tony Perez, Masie Cochran
ASSISTANT EDITOR Thomas Ross

Tin House Magazine (ISSN 1541-521X) is published quarterly by McCormack Communications LLC, 2601 Northwest Thurman Street, Portland, OR 97210. Vol. 16, No. 4, Summer 2015. Printed by Versa Press, Inc. Send submissions (with SASE) to Tin House, P.O. Box 10500, Portland, OR 97296-0500. ©2014 McCormack Communications LLC. All rights reserved. No part of this publication may be reproduced, stored in a retrieval system, or transmitted in any form or by any means, electronic, mechanical, photocopying, recording, or otherwise, without the prior written permission of McCormack Communications LLC. Visit our Web site at **www.tinhouse.com**.

Basic subscription price: one year, $50.00. For subscription requests, write to P.O. Box 469049, Escondido, CA 92046-9049, or e-mail tinhouse@pcspublink.com, or call 1-800-786-3424. Additional questions, e-mail laura@tinhouse.com.

Periodicals postage paid at Portland, OR 97210 and additional mailing offices.

Postmaster: Send address changes to Tin House Magazine, P.O. Box 469049, Escondido, CA 92046-9049.

Newsstand distribution through Disticor Magazine Distribution Services (disticor.com). If you are a retailer and would like to order Tin House, call 905-619-6565, fax 905-619-2903, or e-mail Melanie Raucci at mraucci@disticor.com. For trade copies, contact W. W. Norton & Company at 800-233-4830.

Since our first issue, back in 1999, we have prided ourselves on recognizing new voices. It has been a thrill to discover writers such as Victor LaValle, Justin Torres, and Dylan Landis, and then to watch their careers unfold and blossom. It speaks well of the current literary climate that we are continually surprised and excited by previously unknown writers. For this issue, five New Voices caught our eye. Poets Diana M. Chien and Cody Carvel dazzled us with their energy and wit, while Mary Barnett grabbed our attention with her essay about a decades-old trauma and her continuing struggle to heal. We admired the confidence and precision of the prose in the short stories of Sarah Elaine Smith and Matthew Socia—Smith's "Pink Lotion" following a problematic addiction recovery, Socia's "American Tramplings" being the tale of a stampede epidemic.

While discovering emerging writers is always a thrill, it is a different excitement reading the work of masters who are in full command of their powers. For readers unfamiliar with the latest Nobel Laureate, Patrick Modiano, his "Page-a-Day" (beautifully translated from the French by Edward Gauvin) is an ideal introduction, wherein the author explores his favorite subject—Paris—and obsesses on time, memory, and the legacy of World War II. In "Forgetting Mississippi," Lewis Hyde revisits the brutal 1964 murder of two young black men. Hyde, who was a civil rights activist at the time, not only puts the crime in context but also does the seemingly impossible—searches for forgiveness. Kimiko Hahn, the author of seven volumes of poetry and winner of numerous awards, demonstrates in her four poems how she continues to push her art, reminding us that no matter how accomplished, discovery is experienced poem to poem, word to word. Here's to renewal and discovery.

CONTENTS

ISSUE #64 / SUMMER READING

Fiction

Poetry

||||||||||||||||||||||||||||||||| **Features** |||||||||||||||||||||||||||||||||||

FICTION

Page-a-Day

Not many people out for a stroll yesterday on rue Gay-Lussac. I think I may even have been the only one walking up that gently sloping street, which vanishes at its end into some horizon I no longer recall. Just before reaching the area around les Ursulines I spotted, in a bookstore window, the cover of a book entitled *The Murder of Pierre Bosmans*. A soiled white cover. Right in the middle, a blot of orange with, in black letters, the word MURDER. The cover and the title were in keeping with the Sunday and that street. The next day, I went back to buy the book. It recounted a minor news item. Four young people eighteen years of age, among them a girl, attend the same high school. One fine day, three of them decide to kill the fourth.

Patrick Modiano

translated by Edward Gauvin

The murder is committed by P. one December afternoon, on a wooded path on the outskirts of Paris. What was the motive? Rivalry, since Pierre Bosmans and P. were in love with the same girl. And the four young people lived cut off from reality, in an oppressive atmosphere of pathological lies. Pierre Bosmans had led them to believe he had a fabulously wealthy mistress who lived in the Hôtel de Crillon, that he had two million euros, and that he was a secret agent and an arms dealer.

> **I can still see my father silhouetted there, beneath the entrance, but I can no longer make out his face.**

I wondered if the three accomplices to the crime still lived in Paris now, and what they remembered about when they were eighteen, the nightmare in which they'd wallowed. I pictured them, planning the murder when class let out, on gray days, like that Sunday. They held one last secret council around a café table and their voices were drowned out by the crackle of the pinball machine. They left the café and met up again in a street near rue Gay-Lussac, just as straight and just as cheerless, whose name had a more funereal ring: rue Monge.

• • •

Sunday evenings in winter, the wind blows through place du Panthéon. On the right, lighted windows: the police precinct, one of the most disturbing in all Paris. Yesterday, I thought I was reliving a bad dream. It was time to return to the high school at the far end of the square. I'd been a boarder there at seventeen. Every evening around five, I would see the crowd of students go out the front entrance, and there were but a few of us left in the "recess" courtyard before returning to "study hall." I no longer remember my fellow boarders very well. Sometimes that's how it is for people who've done time in prison: they try to forget their cellmates. Three boys from Sarreguemines were readying for the École Normale Supérieure. A boy from Martinique in my class often hung out with them. Of another student who was always smoking a pipe, and wore a gray coat and carpet slippers, it was said that he hadn't set foot outside school grounds for three years. I also remember, vaguely, the boy one bed over in the dormitory: a little redhead I caught a glimpse of from afar, a few years later, on boulevard Saint-Michel, in a soldier's uniform . . . After lights-out, a night watchman walked up and down the dormitories, lantern in hand, checking if each bed was indeed occupied. It was autumn nineteen hundred sixty-two, but also the eighteenth century, and maybe even an era more remote in time.

. . .

My father came to visit me just once in that institution. The headmaster he'd called to say he'd be passing through had given me permission to wait for him by the front entrance. This headmaster had a pretty name: Adonis Delfosse.

I can still see my father silhouetted there, beneath the entrance, but I can no longer make out his face, as if his presence in this medieval convent setting were somehow unreal to me. The silhouette of a tall, man missing a head.

I can't remember anymore if there was a visiting room. I seem to recall our meeting took place on the second floor in a room that must have been the library, or the function hall. We were alone, seated at a table, facing each other. My father outlined for me the plans he'd made for my future.

He wished me to leave for military service before I was called up. In the four years that followed—until I was no longer a minor—he did not give up on this plan. He wanted to see to all the formalities himself at the barracks on rue de Reuilly. Then off to another barracks, out east.

I accompanied him all the way to the school's front entrance. I saw him walk away across place du Panthéon. One day, my father had confided in me that when he was eighteen, he too hung about the Latin Quarter, with all its colleges. He had just enough money for a café au lait and a few croissants at Dupont-Latin by way of a meal. At the time, he had a shadow on his lung. I close my eyes and imagine him walking up boulevard Saint-Michel, among the well-behaved high schoolers and the students of the far right Action Française. His own personal Latin Quarter was more like the murderess Violette Nozière's. He must have run into her often on the Boulevard. Violette, "the beautiful schoolgirl of Lycée Fénélon, who brought up bats in her desk."

. . .

In 1945, shortly after my birth, my father decides to go and live in Mexico. The passports are ready. But at the last minute, he changes his mind.

He very nearly left Europe after the war. Thirty years later, he went and died in Switzerland, the neutral country. In between, he moved around a great deal: Canada, Guyana, equatorial Africa, Colombia . . . What he sought, in vain, was El Dorado.

. . .

Around 1952, in a little house in Jouy-en-Josas, on rue du Docteur-Kurzenne, I was listening to the radio one Thursday afternoon because of the children's programming. On other days, I would sometimes hear the news report. The announcer gave an account of the trial of the men behind the MASSACRE AT ORADOUR. Today, the sound of those words still chills my heart as it did then, when I didn't understand very well what it was all about.

. . .

One night, during one of his visits, my father is sitting across from me in the living room of the house on rue du Docteur-Kurzenne, by the bay window. He asks me what I would like to do with my life. I don't know how to answer.

. . .

Between Jouy-en-Josas and Paris: the mystery of that suburb not yet a suburb. The ruined château. The meadow. The bois des Metz. The great wheel of the machine de Marly, turning in the roar and chill of a waterfall. The hangars of the aerodrome in Villacoublay. Porte de Châtillon.

. . .

From 1953 to 1956, in Paris, I went with my brother to the local school on rue du Pont-de-Lodi.

. . .

My father was often to be found in his office with two or three people. They would be sitting in armchairs or on the arms of the sofa. They spoke among themselves. They made calls, each in turn. And they tossed the phone to one another, like a rugby ball.

. . .

The mystery of the courtyard of the Louvre, the two squares of the Carrousel and the Tuileries gardens, where I spent long afternoons with my brother. Black stone and the leaves of chestnut trees, in the sun. The theater of greenery. The mountain of dead leaves against the wall at the base of the terrace, below the musée du Jeu de Paume. We'd numbered the pathways. The empty fountain. The statue of Cain and Abel in one of the Carrousel's vanished squares. And the statue of Lafayette in the other. The bronze lion of the Carrousel gardens. The green seesaw against the wall of the terrace at the water's edge. The ceramic and coolness of the "Lavatory" under the Terrasse des Feuillants. The gardeners. The buzz of the lawn

He very nearly left Europe after the war. Thirty years later, he went and died in Switzerland.

mower motor one sunny morning on the lawn by the fountain. The clock with its unmoving hands by the south entrance to the Tuileries Palace. And the red mark of the brand on the shoulder of Milady de Winter.

. . .

Reading books, a few years later. Some left their mark on me:

Fermina Márquez
In the Penal Colony
These Jaundiced Loves
The Sun Also Rises

In others, I rediscovered the magic of the streets:

Marguerite of the Night
Only a Woman
Street Without a Name

In the infirmary libraries of the middle school there were still a few old novels hanging about that had survived the last two wars and stood there, very discreetly, for fear of being taken down to the cellar. I remember reading René Bazin's *The Children of Alsace*.

But above all, I read the pocket paperbacks that were just beginning to appear, especially the cardboard-bound ones in the collection Pourpre imprint. Haphazardly, novels good and bad alike. Many of these have since vanished from backlists. Among these first Livres de Poche, a few titles have retained their mystery for me:

The Street of the Fishing Cat
The Rose of Bratislava
Marion of the Snow

. . .

One Sunday, a stroll with my father and his sidekick of the moment, Stioppa. My father sees him often. He wears a monocle and his hair is so slick with oil it leaves a stain when he rests his head against the back of the sofa. He plies no trade. He lives in a boarding house on avenue Victor-Hugo. Sometimes the three of us—Stioppa, my father, and I—go walking in the bois de Boulogne.

> **Neon-lit cafés on winter mornings when it was still dark out. The hiss of espresso machines.**

Another Sunday, my father takes me—why indeed, I wonder—to the boat fair by quai Branly. We meet one of his friends from before the war: "Paulo" Guérin. An old-looking young man in a blazer. I no longer recall if he too was attending the fair or if he had a booth. My father explains that "Paulo" Guérin has never done a thing besides ride horses, drive fancy cars, and seduce women. Let that be a lesson to me: yes, in this life, you need your diplomas.

That afternoon, my father had a dreamy look about him, as if he'd just seen a ghost. Whenever I found myself on quai Branly, I thought back to the slightly thickened figure of "Paulo" Guérin, with what had seemed a puffy face beneath combed-back brown hair. And the question will forever be unanswered: What could he, without any diplomas, have been doing that Sunday at the boat fair?

. . .

Sometimes on Monday mornings, my father would walk me to la Rotonde by porte d'Orléans. That was where the bus back to middle school awaited me. We would get up around six, and my father would take the opportunity to arrange meetings in cafés around porte d'Orléans before I had to get on the bus.

Neon-lit cafés on winter mornings when it was still dark out. The hiss of espresso machines. The people he met there spoke to him in low tones. Itinerant vendors, men with the ruddy cast of a traveling salesman, or the sly look of a provincial lawyer's clerk. What did they do, exactly? They had earthy names, names of the land: Quintard, Chevreau, Picard . . .

· · ·

One Sunday morning, we took a taxi to the neighborhood by the Bastille and place de la République. My father made the taxi stop twenty-some times in front of apartment buildings on boulevard Voltaire, avenue de la République, boulevard Richard-Lenoir . . . Each time, he left an envelope with the concierge. A call to former shareholders in a defunct company whose stock certificates he'd dug up? The Indochina Mining Union, maybe? Another Sunday, he leaves envelopes up and down boulevard Pereire.

· · ·

On the mantel in his bedroom, several volumes of maritime law, which he studies. He thinks about getting an oil tanker shaped like a cigar underway.

· · ·

Sometimes, Saturday nights, we would visit an old couple, Monsieur and Madame F., who lived in a tiny apartment on rue du Ruisseau, behind Montmartre. On the wall of their little living room, displayed in a frame, the military medal Monsieur F. had won in the War of '14–'18. He had once been a printer. He loved literature. He had given me a handsomely bound edition of Saint-Pol-Roux's collection of poems *The Rose and the Thorns of the Road*. In what circumstances had my father met him?

· · ·

Sunday walks with my father and an Italian engineer, inventor of a patent for "autoclave ovens." My father will also have close ties with a certain Monsieur Held, a "radiesthesist" who always had a pendulum in his pocket.

. . .

An afternoon in June. It was very hot and we were walking—I don't know why anymore—on boulevard de Rochechouart. There, taking shelter from the sun, we'd entered the coolness and dark of a small cinema.

. . .

At night, on his garnet leather phonograph, we would play samples of plastic records he wanted to put on the market.

. . .

One night in the stairwell, my father said something to me I didn't quite understand at the time—one of his rare confidences:

"One must never overlook the small details. Me, unfortunately—I've always overlooked the small details . . ."

. . .

One Monday morning during vacation, I heard steps in the inner stairwell that mounted to my room on the sixth floor. Then, voices in the big bathroom next door. Bailiffs were taking away all of my father's suits, shirts, and shoes. What stratagem had he employed to keep them from seizing the furniture?

. . .

He would have liked me to be an agricultural engineer. He thought it was a trade of the future. If he attached so much importance to schooling, it was because he hadn't had any; he was a bit like those gangsters who want their daughters to be educated at boarding school by "the sisters." He spoke with a slight Parisian accent—from the Hauteville housing estates—and from time to time, used a word or two of slang. But he could inspire confidence in backers, for his style was one of politeness and reserve, a tall man who wore very sober suits.

· · ·

A night in September, 1959, with my mother and one of her friends back from Algiers. We are in an Arab restaurant on rue des Écoles, the Koutoubia. It's late. The restaurant is empty. It's still summer. It's hot. The door to the street is wide open.

Endless days of rain; the covered playground. Turkish toilets.

In those strange years of my adolescence, Algiers was an extension of Paris, and Paris picked up waves and echoes from Algiers, as if the sirocco blew through the trees of the Tuileries, bringing with it a little desert sand. In Algiers and in Paris, the same Vespas, the same movie posters, the same songs in café jukeboxes, the same cars in the streets. The same summer, in Algiers, as on the Champs-Élysées.

That night, at the Koutoubia, were we in Paris or Algiers? Not long after, they bombed the Koutoubia.

Another night, in Saint-Germain-des-Prés, or in Algiers? They'd just bombed Jack Romoli, the menswear shop.

· · ·

September still. Back to school, one Sunday night in the mountains of Haute-Savoie. Recess after lunch; I would listen to the radio. From behind the trees, the shrill and monotonous plaint of the sawmill. Endless days of rain; the covered playground. Turkish toilets.

· · ·

From Annecy, I would take the bus to Geneva, where I was sometimes joined by my father. We would have lunch in an Italian restaurant with one of the men named Picard. In the afternoons, my father had meetings. What a strange place, Geneva. Algerians held long secret councils in the lobby of the Hôtel du Rhône.

I would walk to the old town. On the way back from Geneva, the bus would cross the border at dusk without stopping at customs. Saint-Julien. Cruseilles.

In Annecy, a stroll along le Pâquier when vacation was over. Autumn, already. We would walk by the prefecture, and Annecy would become a provincial town once more. We would run into an old Armenian, always alone; he was said to be a very rich businessman who gave a great deal of money to young girls and the poor.

And Jackie Giroud's gray sports car, designed by Allemano, slowly circles the lake for all eternity.

• • •

Around Christmas 1962, I am taken in by friends in Saint-Lô. The city was obliterated by bombing and rebuilt after the war. By the stud farm, a zone of provisional barracks remains. In the provinces—in Annecy, in Saint-Lô—it was still an era when dreams and nighttime strolls all ended up in front of the station, where a train was leaving for Paris.

> **Queneau's laugh. Half geyser, half rattle. But I have no gift for metaphors. It was quite simply Queneau's laugh.**

In Saint-Lô that Christmas, 1962, I read *Lost Illusions* by Balzac. I was still living in the same room on the top floor of the house. Its window overlooked the highway. I remember that every Sunday, at midnight, an Algerian would walk up the highway toward those barracks, talking softly to himself.

Tonight, Saint-Lô reminds me of the lighted window in *The Crimson Curtain*, as if I'd forgotten to turn the light out in my old room, or my youth.

Barbey d'Aurevilly, beloved of decadents, was born nearby. I'd visited his house.

• • •

In Paris, around the same era, I go over to Raymond Queneau's for Saturday lunch. In the early afternoon, we often take a taxi, and from Neuilly both of us return to the Left Bank.

He tells me about a walk he took with Boris Vian down a little street almost no one knew, somewhere deep in the 13th arrondissement, between quai de la Gare and the railways of Austerlitz: rue de la Croix-Jarry. He recommends it.

Later, whenever we see each other, we will bring up rue de la Croix-Jarry. Some time ago, I read that the happiest moments of Queneau's life had been when he had to write articles about Paris for *L'Intransigeant*, a paper now no more, and he would go walking through the streets in the afternoon.

I wonder if those lifeless years were really worth it. The only moments I was really myself: when I found myself alone in the streets, like Queneau, looking for the dog cemetery in Asnières.

• • •

At the time, I had two dogs. Their names were Jacques and Paul. In Jouy-en-Josas, in 1952, my brother and I had a bitch named Peggy who got run over one afternoon in rue du Docteur-Kurzenne. Queneau loved dogs very much.

• • •

He'd told me of a Western where one witnessed a merciless struggle between Indians and Basques. The presence of Basques had greatly intrigued him and made him laugh. I finally found out the name of the film: *Thunder in the Sun*, a Technicolor Western directed by Russell Rouse, with Susan Hayward, Jeff Chandler, and Jacques Bergerac. The synopsis indeed says: Indians vs. Basques.

I'd like to watch this film in memory of Queneau in a Bikini, Magic, or Neptuna cinema that they've neglected to demolish, somewhere deep in a forgotten part of town.

• • •

Queneau's laugh. Half geyser, half rattle. But I have no gift for metaphors. It was quite simply Queneau's laugh.

• • •

In Paris, spring 1966, I noticed a change in the atmosphere, a climate variation I'd already felt in 1958 at the age of thirteen, then again at the end of the Algerian War. But this time, in France, no significant event, no breaking point—or else I've forgotten it. I would moreover, to my great shame, be incapable of telling you what was going on in the world in April 1966. We were coming out of a tunnel, but what tunnel, I have no idea. And that breath of fresh air wasn't one we'd known in the seasons before.

Was it an illusion of those who are twenty and believe each time that the world begins with them? The air that spring seemed lighter to me.

. . .

To be unflinchingly honest: in 1963, my mother and I had sold, to a Polish man we knew who worked at the flea market, four almost brand-new suits, a number of shirts, and three pairs of Weston shoes with blond wooden shoe trees that a friend of my father's who'd lived with us had left in a closet. He'd vanished overnight in his Citroën DS 19.

That afternoon, we didn't have a dime. At most, change I'd gotten back for bottle deposits from the grocer on rue Dauphine.

After that, I stole some books from people's homes, or libraries. I sold them because I needed money.

. . .

You are in Paris, arraigned before the judge, as Apollinaire said in his poem. And the judge shows me photos, documents, incriminating evidence.

And yet, none of that was my life.

. . .

Spring, nineteen hundred sixty-seven. The lawns of the Cité universitaire. Parc Montsouris. At noon, workers from SNECMA, the aviation company, would come to the café on the ground floor of the apartment building.

Place des Peupliers, the June afternoon when I learned my first book had been accepted.

The SNECMA building by night, like a liner run aground on boulevard Kellerman.

One evening in June, at the Théâtre de l'Atelier, place Dancourt. A curious play by Audiberti: *Heart of Leather*. It was playing only for a few shows.

Roger was working as a stage manager at l'Atelier. The night Roger and Chantal got married, I'd dined with them in a little apartment on that very place Dancourt where shivers the light from streetlamps.

Then they'd left in a car for a distant suburb. I don't know what became of them.

. . .

Perhaps all the people I ran across during those years, whom I've never had occasion to see again, continue to live in a kind of parallel world, sheltered from time, with the faces they had then. I thought of this earlier, walking along the deserted street, in the sunlight.

. . .

Today, May 26, 2001, in the early afternoon, I realized that this gossamer film of gossamer events could tear or attenuate at any minute. I was walking down rue du Val-de-Grâce toward rue Pierre-Nicole. A quiet neighborhood, the Feuillantines. As if the air there were light and kept the echo of years gone by.

"The garden was large, deep, mysterious . . ."

I'd lost all of my life's minuscule landmarks. Scraps of memories flowed through me that were no longer mine, but belonged to strangers, and I could give them no precise form. It seemed I'd lived here once, in a former life. In this place, I'd left someone behind.

Catherine Barnett

THE AUGUST PREOCCUPATIONS

So this morning I made a list
of obsessions and you were on it.
And waiting, and forgiveness, and five-dollar bills,
and despots, telescopes, anonymity, beauty,
silent comedy, and waiting.
I could forswear all these things
and just crawl back into the bed
you and I once slept in.
What would happen then?
Play any film backward and it's elegy.
Play it fast-forward, it's a gas.
I try not to get attached.
But Lincoln!
I see stars when I look at him.

O ESPERANZA!

Turns out my inner clown is full of hope.
She wants a gavel.
She wants to stencil her name on a wooden gavel:
Esperanza's Gavel.
Clowns are clichés and they aren't afraid of clichés.
Mine just sleeps when she's tired.
But she can't shake the hopes.
She's got a bad case of it, something congenital perhaps.
Maybe it was sexually transmitted,
something to do with oxytocin or contractions or nipple stimulation,
maybe that's it, a little goes a long way.
Hope is also the name of a bakery in Queens.
And there's a lake in Ohio called Lake Hope where you can get nachos.
I'm so stuffed with it the comedians in the Cellar never call on me,
even when I'm sitting right there in the front row with a dumb look of hope on my face.
Look at these books: hope.
Look at this face: hope.
When I was young I studied with Richard Rorty, that was lucky,
I stared out the window and couldn't understand a word he said,
he drew a long flat line after the C he gave me,
the class was called metaphysics and epistemology,
that's eleven syllables, that's
hope hope hope hope hope hope hope hope hope hope hope.
Just before he died, Rorty said his sense of the holy was bound up with the hope
that some day our remote descendants will live in a global civilization
in which love is pretty much the only law.

FICTION

Centrifugal Force

Jodi Angel

Harold was off his meds again and we were bored, so we went over and pounded on his door until some guy we'd never seen before opened up and said yeah, Harold was around, and we went in and went looking for him and finally found him out behind the garage, smashing up garden snails with a hammer. There was a shitload of wreckage in front of him—all kinds of shattered pieces and bodies thick and wet as snot—and he was lining more up, one after another, like small brown stones on a junk piece of board, and he would say something, something so quiet and personal that he had to lean in close to the snail to reveal it, and then he would smile and step back, cock his right arm and swing from the shoulder so that we could almost hear the hammer cut through the air, and instead of the sound of metal on wood there was a squelch and shower of shell, and we watched him do this for a while, nobody saying anything, and somebody whispered that maybe we should go find something else to do, but it had rained not that long ago—rained for what felt like weeks—and the sky was still untrustworthy and everybody was broke, and watching Harold bust up snails was about the only thing left to do.

So we just stood around with our hands stuffed deep in our pockets, and somebody had a half-crushed pack of stolen Merits, so we lit a couple up and passed them around and watched the dull sky and Harold, and wiped absently at wet flecks that hit our bare arms or faces because they could have been raindrops or shrapnel. Nobody said anything, and then the sound of the hammer stopped and Harold stood upright and stretched his back and looked at the group of us, gathered around, and Harold said hey, you guys wanna go walking? and we all nodded and Harold rubbed his hammer clean on the patchy lawn and shoved the head into his back pocket so that the handle stuck out like a comb, and we all followed him to the front of the house, and then we were on the street and Harold was in the lead, and we fanned out behind him and when he broke an antenna off a parked car, we all laughed, and then he did it again—snapped one off a green Chevy so that he had an antenna in each hand, and we wondered how many more he might take because there were a lot of parked cars on the street—and we kept laughing until he started whipping at our arms with them—hard—so that the thin metal left behind welts and it was impossible to fend him off—he had one in each hand—but nobody said anything because we were pretty relieved that Harold had forgotten about the hammer, and Harold was heading toward the 7-Eleven and somehow he was always the only one with some money, so we kept walking because we figured it was just a couple of car antennas and Harold was just a guy off his meds, and it was a Saturday in March, and it was getting too late in the afternoon to do something different.

> **Everybody was broke, and watching Harold bust up snails was about the only thing left to do.**

We beat Harold through the store door and we were already grabbing shit to buy because at the very least we should each get one thing, and then somebody said where the fuck is he going? and we all looked up in time to see Harold round the corner outside and cut behind the building—he hadn't even come in—and we stood there for a second, waiting, and then we had no choice but to drop what was in our hands and head out, and there were a couple of eighth-graders on bikes in the parking lot, and we thought about punching them for fun, so we hassled them for a little while and tried halfheartedly to take one of their bikes, but they got all red-faced and rode off, and by the time we crossed the asphalt, Harold was a good block ahead of us and we had to pick up the pace.

The wind had come up in the time it had taken us to walk from Harold's house, and there was a loneliness in it, and we ducked our heads. We used to know Harold when he lived someplace else with his grandma and his dad, but then his grandma died one day and maybe Harold's dad took his dead mother to the bank to sign over a check, and there had been sort of a thing about it in the papers—Harold's dad putting his dead mother in a taxi and then wheeling her through the bank in her chair—her feet falling off the footrests and dragging limp across the floor—and then Harold's dad up and disappeared and Harold stayed in his dead grandma's house for a while, but we figured that probably got boring because Harold moved across town into the house he lived in now with some older guys we didn't know so well. We didn't really know much about Harold either, when we got right down to it—other than what we had heard or seen—but he was sometimes fun to talk to, and he always had some money, and he was willing to do just about anything, and when we went behind the building and walked through the vacant lot, Harold was still swinging the broken antennas ahead of us and he was crossing Jackson Street in the middle of the road.

Get the fuck out of the road, somebody yelled and laid on the horn, and we cut through the tall wet grass and trash that clumped together in the weeds and waited on the sidewalk while Harold kept walking and crossing and then he was on the other side and he was on the bridge now, the one that elevated Jackson Street over five hundred feet above dry riverbed, and he dropped the antennas suddenly, as though he had just realized he was still carrying them, and we could not hear the antennas hit the ground—we just watched them fall and bounce while he kept walking, and then Harold stopped and leaned against the cement guardrail that separated the pavement and the city from the air and the trees, and we figured he was waiting for us to catch up, and maybe he was, but then he jumped up on the rail and stood on the ledge, and there was Harold with his arms out, balanced on the guardrail, walking back and forth, heel to toe, arms extended like wingspan, and a car went by and honked its horn and then another did, too, and Harold shot them both the finger and kept balancing and there was the wind again, pushing us forward so that we crossed Jackson without thinking and we stood there, at the end of the bridge, watching.

Go fuck yourself, somebody from our side yelled, and we laughed because it was an old joke.

Somebody shouted from across the street and we all looked over and saw Hooker Stacy walking on the other side, hands on her hips, and she yelled hey you got a cigarette or hey you want your dick sucked, we weren't sure which, and then she stopped, too, across the street from us, on the other side of two lanes of steady traffic, and she dug through her dirty purse for a minute until she pulled out something and inspected it, put it in her mouth, and then fished a lighter out of the front pocket of her jeans and lit it up, and even though there were cars and noise and she wasn't on our side of the street, we could smell the cigarette within seconds after she exhaled and we all got a craving, but the stolen pack of Merits was long gone.

You should get him down from there, Hooker Stacy yelled. And we all watched her and she was leaning back against her own guardrail now, enjoying the show, and we all tried to ignore her because we had been ignoring her for years.

Go fuck yourself, somebody from our side yelled, and we laughed because it was an old joke, but Hooker Stacy didn't even flinch, and she just stood there, leaned back against the guardrail, pulled on her cigarette, and watched us while we watched Harold and Harold watched the narrow platform underneath his feet.

He's gonna fall, Hooker Stacy yelled back, and we watched her now, took our eyes off Harold for a minute because Harold was Harold and Hooker Stacy was something else. She was older than us, or maybe the same age, but she had never gone to school, and she looked thirty-five on a good day and maybe fifty on a bad one, but there was no sun out today and she was at a distance and from where we stood she could have been clean and young and fresh and we could have pretended that she was somebody different for a while if we wanted to.

We started to cross the bridge to catch up with Harold, but then he changed directions and walked back our way, just turned his feet and spun himself around, left foot over right and he was facing us again, and there was a little bit of dust and a scatter of small rocks as his rubber soles gripped, but we didn't doubt them for a second, and we had only taken a few steps onto the bridge so we shuffled to where we had been standing before, where the ground was still solid, and we waited for him to get to us, but just before he did, he spun around and headed toward the far side again. There was a look on his face that we could not recognize, but it wasn't like we tried, and if it had been a test question, name the look on Harold's face, we would have left the question blank and opted for the next question, about what Hooker Stacy said next, because we all heard it loud and clear—I hope he falls and dies—and her face was an easy read, all smiles—even from this distance—and she kept sucking on the never-ending cigarette and watching us from across the street.

Harold was on the far side now, almost to the other end of the bridge, and we could see the hammer in his back pocket still, the handle against his lower back, tapping in time with each step, and we huddled together and waited to see if Harold would jump off the guardrail when he got to the far side and head toward something else, but he came to a stop long before he got to the end, and we all waited.

He's gonna jump off, Hooker Stacy yelled, and we looked for something to throw at her, but we couldn't find anything except a rock, and it was one thing to hit her, but another thing to hit her hard, so we turned our backs on her and huddled together and waited for Harold to get done because we were hungry and it was getting later and pretty soon it would be dark and there would be better things to do.

Just jump, Harold, Hooker Stacy yelled from across the street, and even though our backs were to her, we could still hear her loud and clear, and we wondered if Harold could too because he was stopped now, completely, and he was almost to the other side, and there was probably enough soft ground to save him even if he did listen to Hooker Stacy and did what she said.

And then it was as if the clouds had been stretched until they were thin and then they split and the rain came suddenly, in big heavy drops, a few at a time, and then the drops halved and separated and halved again so that the small drops pelted us at all angles and we ducked our heads against it and the wind got serious and there were sirens in the distance and part of us wondered if maybe somebody had called them on Harold, and maybe they had, but we could barely see him now, through the rain, and he had gone statue still on the ledge, and we thought maybe he was just waiting it out, and then we saw him reach for the hammer in his pocket and he pulled it out by the handle and held it against his side, and then he took a few steps backward toward the center of the bridge, and then a few more after that, and we watched him, and we thought maybe he might throw his hammer at a passing car, and they were still moving, the cars, with their lights on now, and the sound of their tires sucking wet pavement for grip, and there was a gust of wind and for a second Harold stutter-stepped and we thought we heard Hooker Stacy laugh, but then he caught his balance and there was lightning so that everything lit up quick and this time there was no mistaking it—and then a pickup passed us, going too fast, and we felt ourselves get pushed into each other by the wind and we heard brakes lock up and a squeal and a skid, and we had to turn and look and wait for the satisfaction of metal on metal, but it was nothing but a near miss, and then there was thunder, loud and long, and when we looked back, Harold was gone.

We stood there for a long minute, all of us getting wet and cold, and the traffic kept moving beside us, and across the street, Hooker Stacy had slung her dirty purse over her arm and she was walking in the opposite direction, back toward where we had already been. We yelled to her where's Harold? but she just kept walking as though she couldn't hear, and then she stepped off the sidewalk and onto the vacant lot, walking through the grass and the trash, and we watched her until she got too far in the dark to see.

So for a while we just stood there, thinking maybe that Harold, being Harold, would appear someplace else, someplace farther down the street, and we would hurry to catch up with him, because even Harold was different at night, and it was Saturday night, the best one of the week, and we stood there while the light faded and the rain got weak, and in the splash of headlights we could see everything around us despite the dark—the street and the bridge and the ledge—and we were surprised at so much movement everywhere—it was as though nothing could stay still—even as we stood there and tried as hard as we could to keep the earth from spinning beneath our feet. 🛡

[*THE MAGIC 8 BALL*]

Like *The Magic 8 Ball*, at first I appear vague. Then, when yes-or-no, I am spot-on: *It is decidedly so . . . You may rely on it . . . Signs point to yes . . . My sources say no . . .* But, what was the question and did "good thing we're both married" come into play? *Better not tell you now . . . Reply hazy try again . . . Concentrate and ask again . . .* Though answer eludes, the reply will surface.

[COOTIE]

I'm not unlike a cootie, those from childhood tag since some keep a distance: a student who never took her final, an ex-lover's ex, a colleague who knows that I have the goods on her. But unlike *Cootie*, I pretty much believe everyone except me *is* a cootie with *a beehive-like body, a head, antennae, eyes, a coiled proboscis, and six legs.* Etymology points to Malaysian head lice and WWI trench warfare. I point to corner yoga studio, train station bar, church pew, and his bar mitzvah album. Guess what? *You're it.*

[SORRY!]

Like *Sorry!* I possess that quaternity skill set—Counting, Tactics, Strategy, and Probability—to negate another's progress even while issuing an apologetic "Sorry!" Unlike *Sorry!* I cannot trace origins to Cross and Circle boards, that is, an array of mystical or esoteric designs. True, I very often have designs, such as tricking a student into worshipping Donne or, in my youth, walking the dog but really pouring-my-heart-out on the corner pay phone. True, *I* would revel in being metaphysical. True, I am often apologetic for something I'm certain is not my fault (though I've pretty much gotten over *that* cultural hiccup)! Sorry!

[LIKE WOOLY WILLY]

Like *Wooly Willy*, I was launched in 1955 and I'm still around, less popular and far less cute. Well, unlike Wooly Willy *I was cute!* Unlike that bald guy from Smethport, PA, I've never had dealings with Brunette Betty or Dapper Dan. Also, no beard, mustache, or shaggy eyebrows. (Well, not *shaggy* because severely tweezed.) And I certainly do not live under a bubble. No magnetic wand in my life. And my father never manufactured horseshoe magnets. A slight difference: I was born with a Mongolian spot on my rump, whereas on the reverse side of *Wooly Willy*, the artist's signature is hidden in the grass: *Leonard Mackowski*. Though the face creeped-me-out, I did love to play with that science-cum-magic!

the bus

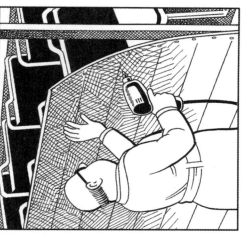

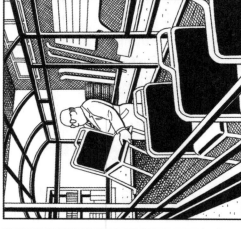
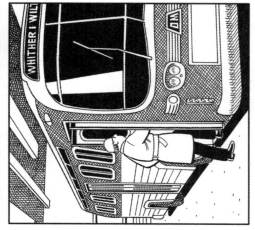

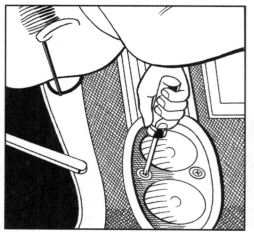

PAUL KIRCHNER

the bus

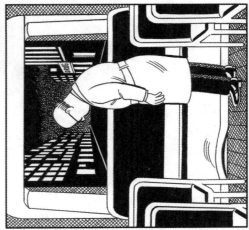

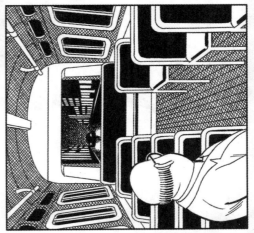

FICTION

The Knitting Story

Tara Ison

She knits as a clumsy, pudge-fingered child, because her mother loves to tell her once-upon-a-time story of knitting socks for her college boyfriend, painstaking argyle wool socks for the princely young man who carelessly thrust his foot through the sock toe after all that labor the mother did to show and prove her love, because that was how. She knits because her mother is at a luncheon or antique show or mah-jongg and Can't the child occupy and entertain herself, and so after school the child trudges to the craft shop and spends her allowance coins on a *Let's Get Knitting!* booklet, and fuzzy pink yarn like a long bubble gum worm, and a pair of pointy twig-thick needles she is a little frightened of, because if you walk around with them and trip you could poke out an eye, and on the floor of her canopy-bed bedroom she teaches herself how to *cast on*, how to loop little nooses of yarn through other loops, scoop the alive loop through, and let the old loop fall away and die, loop loop loop, your rows like little crooked cornfields growing, and then you cast off and are done and look what you have made and can do, ta-da!

She knits gifts for her mother—a pot holder, a hot pad, a long tubular scarf, everything a wormy fuzz pink—because that is how, and her mother exclaims with joy at their sweet misshapenness, and spills bloody meat juice on the hot pad and scorches the pot holder and cannot wear the scarf because of its so-beautiful but impractical color, but is so very proud and What else can the child make, What else can she do?

She knits because she grows absorbed by the taming of chaotic string into structure, the geometry of a messy line turned to a tidy grid, and her fingers slim to deft and she buys slenderer needles and more elegant yarn and her after-schools and weekends are now so very busy herself, in her room with all those squares. Square, square, square, a big gifty pile of them, this is what she can make and do.

She knits because it is precious of her, because grown-ups find this little knitting girl adorable.

She knits because her best friend in high school has prettier ringlet hair and wears girlier, more impractical shoes, and so she teaches her best friend how to cast on and loop loop and cast off, and they both make the now-perfect pot holders, the precise hot pads, the scarves that lie flat, and then the best friend goes away to an expensive college in an icy state and returns at her first Christmas holiday with magical sweaters, glorious garments with plackets and cables and set-in sleeves and stitches like vines and popcorns and the holey appearance of lace that everyone goes *ooh* and *aah* for, and the best friend explains it is not enough to just *Let's Get Knitting!* the same childish stitches over and over again, for row after row gets you nothing but a pile of meaningless squares that no one wants or loves, you must follow a pattern in order to create an actual *ooh* and *aah*

She knits because she grows absorbed by the taming of chaotic string into structure.

thing, and she is angry and ashamed that the prettier, better-shoed, and effortless-at-everything best friend had understood this and she had not.

She knits to perform the trickery with cable needles and yarn overs and ribbing and moss stitch and basket weave. She knits to tame sloppy loose skeins into tidy submissive balls in her hands, at her feet. She knits to exhibit mastery. She knits in public, at coffeehouses and airports and parties, her crafty hands blurred with speed, and people look in approving wonder at her industriousness, her occupying and entertaining herself, her un-idle hands, no lazy devil's handmaiden, she.

She knits because her kneaded dough will not rise into a proper loaf.

She knits because it frightens her to read.

She knits because she can rip out what is imperfect and do *frogging*, the unraveling of the completed or semicompleted thing to an again loose scribble, because you *rip it rip it rip it* out, like the *ribbiting* frog, who is only an ugly sticky frog and not the perfect prince and then you can start all over.

She knits for the first grown-up man she falls in love with, a damaged man whose flattering cruelty sends her to study a library of patterns, swatch multiple yarns, debate even in her sleep the best fiber content and thickness, because the right sweater will heal him, the correct cotton merino or cotton cashmere or cashmere-merino blend will basket weave and moss stitch and cable this man to her, the ribbing will cleave him unto her and keep her at his side, because look at this, her handmade healing labor of love, so she obsesses over this yarn's slight scratch and will it irritate him or keep him sensitized to her, or that yarn's lack of elasticity and will it make of her precious gift a saggy and shapeless thing? She knits because his flattering cruel attentions are trickling hourglass sand, his growing coolness stiffens her fingers, and so she knits faster and even faster, like the princess in the fairy story who races to knit sweaters out of stinging nettles for her twelve beloved brothers turned into swans from a witch's curse and thus turn them back again before they are stuck that unmanly swan way forever, knitting with bleeding fingers to save them into complete-again princes by this show of her love. She knits feverishly, her fingertips pricked into splits, but the sand-gritty time's-up man carelessly thrusts her away before she can finish the last magic stitch, like the fairy tale princess ran out of time and had one sweater with only one sleeve for the swan brother who would now be stuck with one wing instead of an arm forever, and she is consumed with guilt and fury at her failure to craft the perfect healing thing in time, and so she frogs the finished sweater, erasingly, wishing a witch's curse on him, an eternal hair shirt of stinging nettles, a next-in-line indifferent and cruel woman who will brutally cripple and leave him an open, forever-after wound.

She knits vests for the shivering soapy penguins newly cleansed of oil-spill oil, because she is nurturing.

She knits wedding-present blankets for fiancé'd friends, the Victoriana-flowered or Aran fisherman afghans to adorn the feet of marital beds or drape across the Mission sofas in the den or warm their couples' embrace. She knits to soak the DNA from her sweaty fingers into their lives, as they TV cuddle or fuck or share nighttime tales of their tedious stitched-up lives.

She knits because she doesn't like the smell of children.

She knits because she is afraid of her career.

She knits because she is not allergic to cats.

She knits for another man, who is gentle and loving and neither frog nor prince, and she grows impatient knitting for the pattern of his gentle lovingness, she knows nothing she knits will shape him well or into the right thing, so she stealthily unravels her work by night like Penelope's secret unweaving to forestall the choice of a suitor, but by day she keeps on knitting for the gentle loving man, because that is what you do, that is how. She knits like the spider at the center of the web disdains the ensnared fly even as it feeds, she knits in her mind while the gentle loving man makes love to her and she comes only when she imagines herself stabbing her shiny needles into his soft flesh, into the wet submissive ball of his heart, and so she hurries to cast him off and away before she destroys him with her hateful, unmagical knitting, for real.

She knits for pregnant friends' future joys, knits whimsical peapod snugglies and pumpkin hats and the treacle-pink or frozen-waste blue or gender-neutral blankies to be soon covered in apple-juice vomit and leaked urine. She knits for the *ooh* and *aah* baby shower moment of applause, and then it is time for the next, less-wondrous, gift to be opened, and she knits to pity them all.

She knits while watching a television program about people who choose to be cast away on a desert island and contest with each other in mock tribes to remain there, castaway and useful to their tribe in some mysterious strategy for survival, and she knows she would knit hammocks from palm frond strings so everyone might sleep hammock'd up and away from the sand fleas and snakes and rats, she would knit to keep everyone else clothed, she would knit nets to catch fish, and then when all her tribal friends were well-slept and fed and clothed and warm, they would cast her away, cast her off, throw her in a volcano and be rid of her forever.

She knits vests for the shivering soapy penguins newly cleansed of oil-spill oil, because she is nurturing.

She knits sweaters for the naked baby pandas in a Chinese zoo nursery, because she is internationally engaged.

She knits a cardigan for her elderly father, who is already shrinking and shivering inside his closet of clothes meant for a full- and warm-muscled man, but she knits slowly, for she knows that once the sweater is finished he will be too, so she knits stitch by stitch as if patiently teaching a clumsy, pudge-fingered child she doesn't have, until there are no more stitches to stitch and she wraps her father's loose bones in the sweater and buries him in it, because that is how.

She knits security blankets of bargain-bin yarn for homeless abandoned infants, because she is maternal.

She knits chemo caps soft as kitten's bellies for brave, hair-shedding friends with translucent skin, because she is supportive and merciful.

She knits because studies show knitting reduces the risk of dementia, and she will not become a fogged, unraveling person who must rely on mocking, merciless tribal friends for survival.

She knits until her hands are swollen and carpal tunnel'd into witchy old lady knuckle knobs, into burning nerves. She knits into numbness, into scrim.

She knits and knits like Madame Defarge in her chair, content in the breeze of the blade, knits until she feels the blood has risen warm to her ankles and it is suddenly, surprisingly, her turn now, sees she has blindly knitted herself into the wooly smothering thing that will bag her own cold twiggy bones, and that is all she has ever made, or done.

Diana M. Chien

PRIMARY

I have a little lemon soul—
it rests in a china bowl
with red fruit and blue

and then I come back in and
break the bowl and break the fruit
and now the red fruit and the blue
lie with white china slices—
and the lemon slices and slices—
it burns sizzling yellow
at the pretty red round fruit and the dour blue

A SKIN

Skin parkas are not to be trusted. Skin
parkas roam the tundra singly, not in packs.
If you see one standing and waving,
waving from afar, do not go to it.

Skin parkas make a sound like
many things flying;
they can surge like water in spate,
or clap together both

sides sharply—imperious hands.
Stand and watch for long enough the
waving of a skin parka from afar:
you will see this as language, a

semaphore exclusive to arctic dawns
of grey-and-rose tint. The black hole
of the drawn hood: mouth and eye,
equally. O come to me, come.

My son was taken by a skin parka.
He no longer has what I called *son*
inside of him, though his smooth hair
and dark eyes look well enough

in family portraits. Like sleek wood
he sits free from expectation
of presence. Somewhere on the tundra
is a skin parka whose softest

inner fur bears the impress of his face:
life of boy in muffled translation,
it crosses the eye of the arctic sun,
waggles on a strong updraft of cold.

Whole families have succumbed
to skin parkas. Can you see yourself,
a thin skin of memory worn inside?
Grey fur leaks, wavers at the seams.

Paternity

THE CLINIC

You have been trying to start a family. And failing. The problem, it will turn out, is with you. This is what they tell you at the fertility clinic at the medical center. The first thing, discovered during a physical exam, is that your testicles are smaller and softer than average. At the time of this revelation, your wife actually says to the urologist, in a tone of maternal defensiveness: "That's strange, because I would say his penis is a little too big." At which the doctor smiles and explains that the penis is not in question. He gives you a glass vial. Lock yourself in a room where *Playboy* magazines are tastefully fanned out on tabletops and framed prints of Georgia O'Keeffe flowers hang on the walls.

Greg Hrbek

You will have abstained from ejaculation (according to doctor's instructions) for at least two days, but not more than five days, prior to this sample collection. Your apparently undersized balls have been blue. Now, in this weird setting, you'll be damned if you can get an erection. But if you look across the room you will notice a large book: a monograph of erotic art through the centuries. Page through it until you get to a painting called *Naked Young Witch with Fiend in Shape of Dragon*, from the year 1515. The dragon is using a long phallic tongue to penetrate a woman from behind. For some reason, this image will turn you on.

SEXUAL DEFICIENCY IN EARLY AMERICA

Nathaniel Pritchard was a husbandman who, like you, had much trouble impregnating his new wife. Other similarities will become evident. But let us note some differences. Firstly, he was younger than you. Twenty-one at the time of the difficulties, which occurred in the Connecticut Colony of New England in December of 1691. Secondly, he was a farmer: principally of corn, though he also worked a field of rye. As for his wife, Bridget, what her society expected her to be, she was: a weaver, a seamstress, a keeper of chickens. And with her long black hair and pearly skin and eyes the virginal green of an unopened flower, she was all a man from any time could hope to see.

Before the marriage, they bundled.

For twenty-eight nights, in Bridget's girlhood bedchamber, they slept, according to Puritan custom, in separate sheets. Touching only hands and face. Kissing only lips. Nights when desire flourished so powerfully, Nathaniel felt as if floodwaters were threatening to break a dam built at the mouth of his manhood. The barrier did not hold. One morning, he woke in the wee hours, stunned for a few moments that Bridget had unwrapped the blankets and accepted him inside her, before realizing that she was asleep (as he, also, had been asleep) and that his crotch and breeches were wet with ejaculate. Only a dream. Of what the minister would call 'lewd fornication'. He lay awake, the spill between his legs hardening like glue. There was nothing lewd about his love for Bridget—but to have this filthy accident right beside her! Later, bidding her farewell in the crisp outdoors, surrounded by hills of trees whose leaves were blushing and burning with autumn, he said:

'Other young couples in the township do not wait.'

'Ungodly ones,' she replied.

'Godly ones, too. What think you, my love?'

'Methinks you have lost your wits. 'Tis a sin, Nathaniel. You would fain see me whipped at the post?'

'Nay, but— '

She kissed him to stop his mouth. 'Think of me softly,' she said. 'We will know each other soon enough.'

At last, the long-awaited day arrived. They were married by Reverend Moody in a plain service followed by simple refreshments: bridecake; wine and beer; apples and peaches. No dancing, no music. The affair concluded by five of the clock. The late-year sun nearly down when the newlyweds climbed onto the seat of the horse-drawn wagon, and Ezekiel drew them to the cottage at the northern edge of the settlement, where they started a fire in the hearth and ate a dinner of bread and meat—and suddenly, like people awaking from a swoon, found

> **But no matter how he chafed his member it would not erect.**

themselves in the bedchamber, Bridget removing her dress and shift and Nathaniel his shirt and breeches, commencing to touch, to embrace, to treat one another by loving mouth. But even as Nathaniel felt the lust that had tormented him all through the harvest season being transmuted into a divine rapture, something strange and frightful began to happen. Or, rather: strangely and frightfully, something failed to happen. 'My love is such,' whispered his wife, as if reciting a psalm she could not fully remember. 'Communion with thee.' And so lay back, and, draping one arm across her forehead while the other wilted over the bedside, opened her legs. The tallow candle burned: its flame a tiny heart in whose beating Nathaniel could see, about her groin, a down of hair, a sheenful coat of soft fur. 'In the name of heaven,' thought Nathaniel. But no matter how he chafed his member it would not erect. As surely as Christ had died for him, Goodman Pritchard was limp.

AZOOSPERMIA

What the test shows is that you're screwed. Because you have no sperm in your semen. The condition is called azoospermia. You possess a normal libido; you exhibit normal sexual function; and your ejaculate looks like that of any other male. Only it isn't. But there is hope. Because oftentimes men like you do have a "tiny focus" of sperm production in their testicles; and these non-moving sperm can be removed, during a testicular biopsy, via an ultra-micropipette. A single retrieved sperm can then be injected into the woman's egg with a forty-six percent chance of successful fertilization.

Approaching the car after the appointment, your wife will say in a sympathetic tone: "Why don't you let me drive." As if you have been deemed, on top of all else, unfit to operate a motor vehicle.

Don't respond.

Drive the highway and stare through the windshield at the looming skyscrapers of Boston—you who cannot inseminate a female of your species, who just whacked off in a urologist's office to an image that rivals, in its pornographic derangement, anything accessible on the Internet.

> **In the morning, make the appointment. Schedule a time to get a needle stuck into your nut sack.**

"Honey," she will say.

"What."

"It'll work. There's a sperm in there. The Little Zoa That Could."

"What if he can't?"

"Look, I know you're scared of the needle."

"It's not the needle. It's— It's the whole thing. Having a baby that way."

"What."

"I don't know. It's not natural."

"It grows in me," she'll say. "They put the egg back in me and the baby grows natural as can be."

That night, lie in the dark and think about how you and your wife have been mating like animals for a year with never a snowball's chance in hell of her getting pregnant; and how you agreed, back when you were dating—before the wedding day, before the engagement, before the proposal—that you would have children.

Soon.

In the morning, make the appointment. Schedule a time to get a needle stuck into your nut sack.

THE DISAPPEARANCE

And so it went for a fortnight. For two week did Nathaniel lie with Bridget and try to erect himself, and she to erect him with all manner of allurements to venery. But night after night, Goodman Pritchard suffered the same dreadful weakness—until, on the morning after the fourteenth failure, something more than weirdish, something unnatural and unspeakable befell him.

A cold winter morning.

He rose before his wife, whom he could not see at all in the shuttered darkness of the bedchamber, though he could see the phantoms of his own breath, and could, in his mind, judge the way and distance to the door. In the common room of the cottage, a few embers were still glowing in the hearth. (He'd been up in the night to tend the fire.) Now he laid some kindling on the hot remains of cedar wood. Then pulled on a cloak and stepped into his boots and went outdoors. To urinate. The air was bitter; stars were spread like a hoarfrost on heaven; and as Nathaniel walked over the icy ground toward the privy, he thought of the night before—of how, once again, he had tried to do his duty as a husband, and had failed, and finally had buried his face shamefully in his wife's bosom and wept.

Now he opened the door of the privy. Stepped in. Unbuttoned his breeches and reached inside the flap. And felt . . .

Nothing.

For a long moment, Goodman Pritchard did not understand, experiencing, like a man at market feeling in vain for the coins which are never *not* in the pocket of his coat, more perplexity than panic. Then, all at once, a feverish heat flamed over him; and with shaking hands, he pushed down his underclothes and touched all about the crux of himself—and touched nothing but an absence. His mind capsized. 'In God's name,' he choked out. Going to his knees. To pray to the Saviour, one might think. Though one would be mistaken. For to the poor husbandman, dizzy now with terror, it seemed not impossible that the things he was missing might have simply fallen to the floor.

'Nathaniel?'

It was the sweet voice of his new wife, who through the fortnight of his impotence had been nothing if not gentle and kind. But *this*. How could Bridget fathom this? How could he explain—

And then: the cold blast of a different question that turned the goodman's blood to ice:

Am I witched?

Aye, it stands clear. Someone in unholy covenant with the powers of the dark hath stolen your member.

INTRA CYTOPLASMIC SPERM INJECTION

Of course they numb the scrotum; and as the anesthesia takes effect, you will have a sense that your testes are fading out of existence—although, like an amputee who claims to feel the phantom of a missing limb, you think you can feel the needle go in. From your wife, several ripe eggs, clustered like caviar in the ovaries, have already been harvested, and are waiting in a lab room for your sperm. A few of which are found. Hiding in the seminal depths. Girl-afraid introverts who can't swim, and who hold for dear life onto the apron strings of your little nuts while the fluidic riptide of the needle rages all around them. In the laboratory—which you imagine to be white and rectilinear and devoid of sound, a set from a movie about a future world in which, beneath the flawless exterior of scientific advancement, lurks a terrible secret—the reproductive endocrinologist will microinject a single sperm into each of the four oocytes. A day later: good news. Fertilization and cell division are underway. Return to the clinic. In a white silent room, hold your wife's hand while she opens her legs and a catheter is inserted into her vagina.

That night, she will drape her body in white lingerie that gives her the look of an angel about to fall from grace.

Ask: "What are you doing?"

"Sexing up."

"I don't think that's a good idea. What if we break it?"

She laughs. "What do you think it is, a dinner plate? I read about this in a book. Make love when they transfer them."

So, do it—but be warned: the transaction will be a strange one, because you will feel like actors attempting to convince an audience that you're doing something you're actually not doing; and yet the whole thing will make both of you uncommonly hot, as if this pretense of knocking someone up is a fantasy you get off on, though of course it's nothing *but* a fantasy—the implications of which will make you angry and spark the kind of erotic fracas that characterized your early fucks, complete with forcible restraint, slapping, and sexual slurs, until finally, sobbing with want, she will get on all fours. Offering her back parts. The position reminds you of the painting from the book in the urologist's office. The witch and the demon. When the orgasm finally comes, she presses her face to the bed and screams.

DRINKING AS COMPULSIVE BEHAVIOR

The truth is that, for quite some time, for weeks before his sudden and unbelievable castration, Goodman Pritchard had been a frequent, almost nightly, patron at the Anchor, an "ordinary" kept by a friend, Jacob Armitage. A penny for an ale-quart of beer. Which Nathaniel would drink by the fire while staring into the flames and listening to the sound of vapours escaping from the burning fuel: a sinister hiss.

In those days, a man was forbidden to continue tippling above the space of half an hour; but on the night of the day on which he lost his manhood, Nathaniel Pritchard had been in the taproom of the Anchor for nearly an hour already when he said: 'Pray, another ale.' To which Goodman Armitage, the keeper of the tavern on that road that joined Boston to Stamford, replied: ''Tis past nine of the clock.' But Nathaniel professed not to care about the commandments of, or the punishments threatened by, the General Court of Connecticut. Cannot a man quench a thirst without he pay a fine. Et cetera. To quiet him, the innkeeper brought him another beer, and stood by while Nathaniel drank a long draught. The fire cracked and hissed. The two were alone in the taproom.

In the glowing coals he perceived an impression of hell. Fear outweighed shame.

'Nathaniel, what ails you?'

'I know not.'

'And I believe you not.'

Goodman Armitage seated himself. Nathaniel drank another draught and looked into the fire. His brain was bobbing on drink like a cork on water. In the glowing coals he perceived an impression of hell. Fear outweighed shame. He confessed to his friend everything: about the nights of bundling and the episode of nocturnal pollution; about the night of his wedding and the weakness in his penis that had lasted ever since; and how, finally, just this morning, he had waked and gone out to the privy and found—found that it wasn't there at all . . .

'The privy?' said Jacob.

'No.'

'Man, surely you can't mean . . .'

'Aye, I do.' Tears dripped down Nathaniel Pritchard's cheeks, hot as wax down the shaft of a candle molded by the hand of his newlywed wife. 'What think you, Jacob?'

'Be it—Be it there now?'

Sniffling, wiping his face on his sleeve, Nathaniel shook his head. Looked his friend at last in the eye, hoping . . .

He knew not what.

Goodman Armitage said: 'Show me.'

'I'd as lief not.'

'Nathaniel, mark me. I think you be somewhat bewildered. If your claim be true, we shall go straightaway to the reverend, for conjuration be the only conclusion. But I pray you, let us touch the bottom of this.'

Goodman Pritchard stood up. Stood before Goodman Armitage in the taproom of that tavern at the crossroads. He loosed his trousers and let them fall. Then he summoned all the will in his person and pushed down his breeches.

> Suffice to say, your wife's only hope of growing a baby in her womb rests with the semen of a third party.

'What see you?'

'What *see* I? I see your yard, man. Plain as day.'

When Goodman Pritchard put a hand between his legs, he could feel none of himself. 'It is not there.'

'Nathaniel. It will take no prize, but it sufficeth. Now, I pray you,' the innkeeper said, confiscating the tankard, 'get you home to your wife—and use your member for that which God gave it you.'

YOUR LESBIAN FRIEND

Fast-forward to the winter of the year. By which time the sperm injection procedure will have failed. Twice. Leaving two frozen embryos. The doctors defrost them: one does not survive the warming. Have the last transferred to your wife's uterus. A week later, the blood will come. Examine the stain together. Like a pattern left by tea leaves. Not difficult to read the meaning. You know what is coming next. The idea frightens you and twists your stomach into jealous knots. Still, as your wife drops the underwear into the trash and sits on the toilet in an attitude of unconditional surrender, there will be an urge to speak of it, to agree to it . . .

Don't.

This is no time to be rushing into such a thing. You have to get your head straight. You need advice.

Next day, show up at a local pub. Sit at the bar and order a beer with a high alcohol content. Wait for your friend, whom you think is the ideal confidante. She is a beer connoisseur, she's married, and she's the parent of a child, a two-year-old boy, conceived with donated sperm. Here she comes, in the usual attire: a collared shirt tucked into trousers. At her wedding, she wore a tuxedo.

Say, after some small talk: "Did you guys ever consider adoption?"

"Yes."

"But you wanted . . . "

"Kara wanted," she says, bringing her glass to her lips. She is a woman of words so few and precise that you sometimes feel, in conversation with her, that you're talking to a well-coached witness. Tell her, straight up, that you currently find yourself in a position she will understand. Don't embarrass her with the details. Suffice to say, your wife's only hope of growing a baby in her womb rests with the semen of a third party . . .

Lull in the bar.

As if the words have been transmitted, on some drunken frequency, to the ears of all patrons.

Your friend will say: "I don't understand these women."

Nod in assent.

"It's like temporary insanity," she says. "They become convinced they have to experience the thing. If they don't, life is . . . meaningless. So what's marriage? Is marriage just a presupposition?"

"But you agreed."

"True."

"And . . . "

"And it's over and I love Eli. He's half Kara and that's all I think about now. It's all I care about."

On the way home, think only of your wife. Filter out all thoughts of *him*, who in a way is no one, who will be nothing more than a list of physical traits and genetic data: neither enemy nor friend; never to be seen or heard from; all but nonexistent. It is nearly ten o'clock when you open the door. Call out a hello. You will find her on the bed with a glass of wine and a book. Swallow your heart. Tell her. You'll do whatever is necessary. There's no option you won't consider.

CONTRACT WITH SATAN

And so did Goodman Pritchard find himself in a great strait. Unable to tell anyone else of his affliction, for he knew they would seem to see what most assuredly had vanished; and unable even to attempt communion with his wife, for how could he enter her if he had no means? He did not return to the tavern those next three night, but sat by the hearth in his home, feeding the fire, watching flame consume wood.

'Nathaniel,' said Bridget on the third night.

'Aye.'

''Tis past ten of the clock. Will you not come to bed?'

He did not answer, expecting her, as she had done two nights past, to withdraw passively into the bedchamber.

She did not.

But stood in the doorway for a long time while he gazed into the fire. Finally, she said: 'I think you like me not, Nathaniel. To tell you true, I am entirely amazed. Wherefore marry me, if only to keep such cold company?'

He couldn't speak. The fire burned. And still, Goodwife Pritchard stood on the threshold of the bedchamber.

'Hear me now, Nathaniel. Do you hear me?'

'Aye.'

'I want not a pretended husband.'

It was much later, toward midnight, when he quit the cottage and hitched the horse to the cart.

The land of Goodman Pritchard, one hundred acres of it, lay by the northern border of the village, not far from the road that led to Boston. Very near the wilderness—and very soon was he in the wilderness. In a sea of trees that seemed endless. In whose infinitude lurked wild animals, and savages more wild than animals, and, aye, agents of the Devil. On that winter night, as he steered his wagon farther and farther from the village, deeper and deeper into the forest, Nathaniel was affrighted by all such danger and evil. But more affrighted was he by the spectre of a shame to which the embarrassments of the last month would pale in comparison. For in those days, it was well known—suggested both in books of advice and by the laws of the colonial courts—that a man's domestical duty was to make his wife's womb skip with joy. So, Nathaniel was terrified now: not only of the real possibility of being called before the reverend and the village elders to answer for his failures but also of the prospect of losing Bridget, in whose bosom his heart had long taken up its lodging, and of a future in which he would be all alone, with no woman and no children . . .

He pulled on the reins.

The horse slowed and stopped. The goodman had reached a very dark place. Where the road was scarcely visible. Where the trees, though stripped naked by the season, blocked the light of the waxing moon, for the upper branches had come to intertwist—and when Nathaniel looked up, he believed the boughs overhead to be writhing like serpents in a nest. And how cold it was! Scarcely did a tear drop from his eye before it turned to ice. He wiped the crystal from his cheek. And then, in the frozen silence of that place, where no sound had yet come to Nathaniel's ears but that of his own heart—and certainly he had heard no footfalls—a voice said from very near:

> And how cold it was! Scarcely did a tear drop from his eye before it turned to ice.

'Hello, friend. You have some few queer questions. Come down and walk with me, and we will speak on it.'

THE WEBSITE

Open an account. Decide upon a password. Confirm it. Choose a lost-password question. You can now begin to search for donors by selecting attributes. Ethnicity; height; education level; ancestry. The fathers-to-be have no proper names, only numbers. Donor 11936. Making you think of some science-fictional dystopia in which all procreation is controlled by an evil cryobanking corporation that exploits a genetically engineered work-force of breeders. Pay for a Level III subscription and gain access for ninety days to extended profiles, facial feature reports, and childhood photos.

Here is the plan:

You and your wife will search the profiles separately, choose ten donors, and see if you make any choices in common.

Late one night, fifth of bourbon in reach, visit the website. Thinking, while the home page invites you to narrow the search: Christ, even *this* online. Select the skin, hair, and eye colors corresponding to your own. Then ask yourself: Why the same colors? What is the goal here? To blur the line between you and the genetic father and so secure a future unfraught with suspicions and questions? Click on a profile. Picture of a four- or five-year-old with thick shiny hair and a winning smile, a boy destined to grow up and get paid to shoot his load into a glass tube that can now be purchased for a price between 119 and 479 dollars (US) depending on motility—i.e., number of sperm with normal forward movement that will soon be in your wife's fallopian tube and storming the plasma membrane of her ovum, each carrying within itself a familial history of health/physique/intelligence that will (assuming one of them breaks through) merge and blend with that of your wife to form a new human destiny with zero chromosomal input from you.

> See how similarities continue to accrue. Each of you has done something you don't want the world to know about.

In the end, reach a kind of agreement. Green eyes. Average build. Education: Bachelor's degree with departmental honors. Musical instrument: Trumpet. Paternal grandmother: Artist. Favorite color: Cerulean. Number of mobile spermatozoa per milliliter after thawing: Twenty million.

CONCEPTION

And the word of the evil one did prove good. For Nathaniel, on his return from the forest, passed neither cart nor rider; and upon emerging from the trees and coming in view of his frozen fields, saw no wood smoke rising heavenward from the chimney of his cottage. He stabled the horse. Entered the house. Indeed, his wife was still asleep. He laid a log on the embers in the hearth; and with a few breaths directed at the bed of glowing coals, brought the fire to life. He removed greatcoat, then boots. And touched *there*. Aye. The bargain he had struck in the forest was no dream.

Not only was his member returned to its rightful place—it was erected, and as solid as the rock upon which the Lord had built His Church.

On that morning—and many times more through the grey and cold winter of 1692—did Nathaniel fulfill his nuptial duty (on one blessèd occasion inspiring in Bridget's privy parts three successive pangs of pleasure) until at last, three month later, just before the thaw . . .

'My husband.'

'Aye?'

They were at table, enjoying a supper of pork and turnips with cups of fermented cider. A tallow candle burning between them.

'I wonder if you have suspicioned anything of late.'

'I know not.'

Even in the dim light, the bloom in her cheeks was unmistakable. 'When we last . . . conversed. Noticed you no change in me?'

'Let me think on it,' he replied.

But sure he knew. It had happened, as he knew it would. As the Infernal Chymist had guaranteed. His wife was with child. By Nathaniel's reckoning, she would be delivered somewhere about summer's end—on which day a kind of hourglass would be turned, and sand begin to trickle through the neck. A fortnight. Such were the terms of the hellish compact. Signed in his own blood. Within a fortnight of the birth day must Nathaniel Pritchard return to the forest. Not alone: with his newborn child. He wasn't sure which amazed him more. That he was soon to be a father. Or that he had sworn to do a thing that no Gospel Christian would ever dream of.

EARLY DECISIONS ABOUT OPENNESS

See how similarities continue to accrue. Each of you has done something you don't want the world to know about. (Of course, if *you* confide in someone, that person is unlikely to set in motion a series of events resulting in your being publicly burned to death. But this is a question for historians.) What you have to do is sit down with your wife, whose belly, entering into this second trimester of pregnancy, is in a state of erotic distension—filled, you cannot stop yourself from thinking, by *him*—and make a list of people open-minded and discreet enough to be candidates for membership in an "inner circle." Listen to her nominations, which will include parents, siblings, pals from college, childhood BFFs—and realize there is not a single living soul to vote for. Not one. If she says you're being unreasonable, she does have a point. However, reason is only part of the picture. Other forces in operation here include: will, emotion, imagination. If you are going to be a father—a real father—you must believe you are one, and must lose yourself in a story of fatherhood, to a point maybe where you almost forget the thing that began the story, in the sense that it becomes so irrelevant over time that, for all intents and purposes, it never happened.

Attempt to explain your position in these terms. She, after giving you a long look teetering on the edge of patience, will close her eyes, shake her head, and, unlocking her phone, proceed to check messages.

INFANT MORTALITY

All through that spring and summer of 1692 were the dreams of Nathaniel Pritchard corrupted. He would return to the cottage after a day of ploughing or sowing to find his sweet wife in the kitchen, belly full of child, humming a hymn tune, and he would eat the evening meal with her, speaking on topics such as the making of a cradle or the choosing of a name—afterwhich, frighted, he would carry these notions into sleep, where they would be made monstrous by the powers of the dark.

Day by day did the baby grow in the womb; in the fields grew the flint corn and rye. Until, one Indian summer morn after the harvest, the pains began. In accord with custom was the father sent away. He took an axe and went as far as he could, all the distance to the northern fence—and while the neighborhood women fed the mother eggs and broth and cheerfully conversed in support of her spirits and held her on the birthing stool as she moaned and pushed, the goodman set to clearing a new acre, swinging the tool against the trees, chopping for hours with all his angry might until at last, near to three of the clock, the midwife's daughter came stumbling across the fields, calling out: ''Tis finished, goodman! 'Tis a girl!' The news struck hard upon him. If a boy, the task would be terror enough. But a girl. Like a man walking to the gallows, he walked back to the cottage—and he entered the bedroom and saw his sleeping wife and his infant child asleep on her breast, and he sat by them until the sun went down, thinking, as darkness fell over New England: 'Child. Dear child . . . '

Pray, judge him not. For in those days there was a moving plot in the country and scarce did anything happen but the Devil be in it somewhere. It was merely one child. Who might in the normal course have been lost to any number of ills or accidents. Over the next twelve year, there would be between Nathaniel and Bridget much corporeal communion. Six more children would she bear (two would die before speaking a word), but not a single one without the first had served as payment. It may move you little that Nathaniel Pritchard cried an ocean of salt tears the night he stole his firstborn and took her into the forest. But he did cry an ocean. As he would each year thereafter, on the anniversary of that September day. For always on that day did Nathaniel go into the forest, into that realm of abominations, with a garland of wildflowers to lay upon the spot where he had stood that night in 1692, holding the baby in his arms, smelling her milkbreath, waiting for the bootheel of Lucifer.

The news struck hard upon him. If a boy, the task would be terror enough. But a girl.

DREAMS AS CLUES TO HIDDEN PATTERNS

You are in this dark forest. And you're naked. Whatever. Ever since your diagnosis, your dreams have pretty much been clothing optional: you've been buck naked in the supermarket, at the office, in the church you went to as a kid—and now in a strange forest in the middle of the night. At least this time no one can see you. Whoever *was* here is going away—in what sounds like a horse-drawn cart. Clopping hooves, circumvolving wheels. Fading, fading, gone. Leaving you completely alone. Or maybe not. Because it suddenly comes into your head that you're here to help someone . . .

Find her lying at the base of a tree. Swaddled in a blanket of loom-spun wool. Asleep.

Lift her up.

No sooner will her tiny head come to rest on your chest than you will be torn away from that world. Wake up. The baby—the real one—is crying. Squint at the numbers on the clock. Your wife will nudge you in the small of the back. Your turn. As you go to the crib, the dream is forming again, like a wave, in the deep of your mind, now cresting, now crashing. For a few seconds, you are in that forest again. Holding the baby. She isn't yours. She belongs to someone else. Someone long gone into a darkness outside the scope of your subconscious. But you. You are there for her now. In the dream it all makes perfect sense. She called out to you. From far off. Across dimensions, with a silent voice you were somehow able to hear. Of all the men in the world, she called for you. ⛨

FORGETTING
MISSISSIPPI

Lewis Hyde

Getting past the past

I do not remember how I got to Mississippi. I know I started from my parents' home in Rochester, New York, and that I went first to Memphis. My parents had stalled my departure, insisting I come home from college before going south, so I missed the initial 1964 Freedom Summer orientation in Oxford, Ohio, and instead attended a second in Tennessee.

I think I took a bus. And I think I had a several-hour layover in Columbus, Ohio, and that I went to a burlesque show at which I was disappointed to find nothing very sexy on display. I was eighteen.

The thousand or so volunteers who traveled to Mississippi that summer did so to register black voters and to help organize the Mississippi Freedom Democratic Party in hopes of unseating the all-white delegation that the state's Democrats would inevitably be sending to the party's August nominating convention.

Inspired by Martin Luther King Jr.'s "Letter from Birmingham Jail," I had, while still in Rochester, responded to an editorial in the local paper with an idealistic letter to the editor announcing that "injustice anywhere is a threat to justice everywhere." My father, having read the letter, advised me that one trick to good writing was to cut the flamboyant parts (racism was "like a boil," I'd written, and "the pus must continue to drain," etc., etc.), but it was too late—I had posted my manifesto.

Other than the disappointing burlesque show, I remember nothing of the trip. The orientation in Memphis must have been on a college campus; I remember a basement classroom where a man named Staughton Lynd taught us something. Perhaps I got to Laurel, Mississippi—where I was to work all summer—on another bus, or perhaps we took a bus to Jackson, then drove to Laurel. It's all lost.

Or rather it's lost from memory but not from history, for luckily Mother and Father kept the letters I wrote that summer so I have documents to supplement recollection's shabby record. I *did* take a bus and the trip was a twenty-nine hour "torture." The Memphis orientation was

at Le Moyne College; a "strange fellow," Richard Beymer, "the guy who played Tony in *West Side Story*" was in the group; Staughton Lynd taught us that the "Removal Statute of 1868," under which "a case can be removed from the state courts to fed courts," might be invoked when we got arrested but that it was "more of a stall than a workable means." When I got to Laurel we tried to rent a car and the local Avis outlet offered us a hearse; I read a book by "Bert. Russell," whom I described to my parents as a "very cool cat." The three-page mimeographed "SECURITY HANDBOOK" we were given warned: "When getting out of a car at night, make sure the car's inside light is out," to which I added in pen: "unscrew it."

Of all my scattered and fragmented memories from that summer, one in particular stands out: when Lyndon Johnson sent four hundred sailors into the state to walk the swamps and drag the rivers searching for the bodies of three volunteers—Mickey Schwerner, James Chaney, Andrew Goodman—murdered by the Klan on June 21, these sailors found other bodies, dead men no one had been looking for, no one had reported missing. "So this is Mississippi," I thought, a place where a walk through any swamp might uncover the invisible dead, unnamed, unsought.

Last year, I decided to see if there was any truth to this memory. I began searching the *New York Times* online and on microfilm. The reading was slow: other events drew my attention (Barry Goldwater was running for president, the Vietnam

War was on the horizon) and the papers were voluminous (Sunday editions ran to hundreds of pages). I worked for several days and found much about the missing volunteers but nothing about other bodies. Perhaps this was a false memory, or a rumor that we circulated that summer, a projection of our fears.

. . .

Forgetfulness in Greek is *lêthê*, in turn related to *letho* ("I escape notice; I am hidden"), *ultimately from a Proto-Indo-European root meaning "to hide."* The privative or negative form of this word, *a-lethe* or *aletheia*, is usually translated as *truth*, the truth then being a thing uncovered or taken out of hiding. In terms of mental or cultural life, all that is available to mind is *aletheia*; what is not available is for some reason covered, concealed, hidden.

In this tradition, then, to forget is to hide, to conceal, to cover up. And here I imagine a folk etymology and suggest that this covering up is also burial. And that, to begin to sketch the scope of forgetting in regard to personal or cultural trauma, there are two kinds of burial: in one, something is hidden because we can't stand to or refuse to look at it; in the other, it is buried because we are done with it. It has been revealed, examined, and now it may be covered up

> I worked for several days and found much about the missing volunteers but nothing about other bodies.

or dropped for good. The latter is proper burial, burial after... and funeral rites observed... has been paid

. . .

Cranking through the old newspaper microfilm, looking for coincidentally discovered murder victims, I finally came upon a UPI report dated July 12 that told how "a fisherman found the lower half of a body, its legs tied together, floating in the Mississippi River." It seemed that Mickey Schwerner had been found: "It was the body of a white man," the UPI declared; "the belt buckle carried the initial 'M'" and there was a gold watch in the blue jeans pocket. "Civil rights workers . . . said Mr. Schwerner had a gold watch."

So I had misremembered. A body found in the river, not a swamp. Near the Delta, not in Neshoba County. A white, not a black, man.

But no, the news from the following day corrected the story. The body of Charles E. Moore, a black youth from Meadville, Mississippi, had been found, so badly decayed that his race was not apparent. And a second body had been found nearby, that of Henry Dee, also young and black, also from Meadville. The boys had been missing since early May. "Rope and wire found around their bodies indicated they had been bound and thrown into the river."

After this, however, the New York Times here is hardly another on Dee and Moore until the following winter, when three short articles appeared: November 7: "2 Whites Seized in Negro Slayings"; November 8: "2 Whites Released on Bond in Killings"; January 12: "Whites Freed in Slayings."

James Ford Seale and Charles Marcus Edwards, both members of the Ku Klux Klan, had been arrested and charged with willful murder. Their families posted bond; the men were released; at a January hearing the charges were dismissed, the Franklin County DA saying that "additional time" was needed to solve the case.

\

· · ·

In Mississippi in those days, the White Knights of the Ku Klux Klan believed that they were Christian soldiers opposing the forces of Satan on this earth and that the civil rights workers invading their state were the newly fashioned betrayers of Jesus the Galilean. The Imperial Wizard of the Mississippi Ku Klux Klan, Sam Bowers of Laurel, part owner of a jukebox and vending machine company called Sambo Amusement, had devised a secret code to tell his crusaders when to burn a cross or to whip a man or to firebomb a church or to eliminate a heretic, eliminate him without malice, in complete silence,

and in the manner of a Christian act. In Mississippi in those days, the White Knights of the Ku Klux Klan believed that young Negro men had signed agreements promising to rape, weekly, one white woman, that there was an impending Negro insurrection, that the Black Muslims in Chicago had smuggled five thousand automatic weapons, "and maybe a machine gun," into the state and had hidden them in churches and graveyards. In Greenville, Mississippi, the Klan persuaded Washington County deputies that by the act of "felony grave tampering" these guns had been hidden in the cemetery of a black church. "Working in the dark, foggy graveyard, heavily armed police pried the lid from a wooden vault," finding no guns but disturbing the rest of one James Turner, only recently buried.

> Every act of memory is also an act of forgetting. Such, at least, was one ancient understanding.

· · ·

Every act of memory is also an act of forgetting. Such, at least, was one ancient understanding. In Hesiod, the mother of the Muses, Mnemosyne, is not simply Memory, for even as she helps humankind to remember the Golden Age she helps it to forget the Age of Iron it now must occupy. Bardic song was meant to induce those twin states: "For though a man have sorrow and grief . . . yet, when a singer, the servant of the Muses, chants the glorious deeds of men of old and the blessed gods who inhabit Olympus, at once he forgets his heaviness and remembers not his sorrows at all." In this conceit, both memory and forgetting are dedicated to the preservation of ideals. What drops into oblivion under the bardic spell is the fatigue, wretchedness, and anxiety of the present moment, its unrefined particularity, and what rises into consciousness is knowledge of the better world that lies hidden beyond this one.

Left to Right: Charles E. Moore and Henry Dee

• • •

On Saturday, May 2, 1964, Charles Moore and Henry Dee, both nineteen years old, were hitchhiking across from the Tastee-Freez on the outskirts of Meadville, Mississippi. Moore was a student at nearby Alcorn College, at the time suspended for joining a protest about the lack of social life on the campus. Dee worked at a local sawmill. Neither had any involvement in the civil rights movement.

James Ford Seale of the Bunkley Klavern of the Ku Klux Klan picked the boys up and took them into the nearby Homochitto National Forest, where he and four other Klansmen tied them to a tree and beat them savagely with sapling branches. Dee had recently returned from a trip to Chicago; he wore a black bandana: surely he knew where the guns being smuggled into the state were hidden. One of the Klansmen, Charles Marcus Edwards, asked if the boys were "right with the Lord," the implication being that they were about to die. In desperation, one of them invented a story: yes, there were guns—they were hidden in Pastor Clyde Briggs's church over in Roxie.

The Klansmen split up, one group going to the courthouse in Meadville to get Sheriff Wayne Hutto to go with them to Briggs's church (where they found no guns). The others took the beaten boys to a nearby farm. They were bleeding so profusely that the Klansmen spread a tarp in the trunk of a Ford sedan before stuffing the boys into it and driving them ninety miles north to Parker's Island, a backwater bend of the Mississippi River.

When they opened the trunk they were surprised to find the boys alive. One of the men asked if they knew what was going to happen. They nodded. James Ford Seale taped their mouths shut and their hands together. He bound their legs with rope and wire. He and another man chained Henry Dee to a Jeep engine block, loaded him into a boat, rowed him out onto the river, and rolled him into the water, alive. Charles Moore watched from the shore.

The men returned, chained Moore to another weight, rowed him out onto the river, and rolled him into the water, alive. Later they were to say that they dumped Dee and Moore alive rather than shoot them because they did not want to get blood all over the boat.

· · ·

Says Tiresias to Creon, who will not properly bury the body of Polynices, now lying outside the gates of Thebes, picked at by carrion birds and dogs:

"As I took my place on my ancient seat for observing birds . . . I heard a strange sound among them, since they were screeching with dire, incoherent frenzy; and I knew that they were tearing each other with bloody claws, for there was a whirring of wings that made it clear. At once I was alarmed, and attempted burnt sacrifice at the altar where I kindled fire; but the fire god raised no flame from my offerings. Over the ashes a dank slime oozed from the thigh bones, smoked and sputtered; the gall was sprayed high into the air, and the thighs, streaming with liquid, lay bare of the fat that had concealed them.

"Such was the ruin of the prophetic rites."

· · ·

The Klansman who owned the boat used in the murders of Dee and Moore had a brother who knew nothing about their drowning. But this man felt he should tell his brother what had happened because at the point where the brother frequently crossed the river he had the habit of dipping up water to drink and he should be warned that he was "drinking water off a dead Negro."

· · ·

In the Dee-Moore murder case, historical memory—the contemporary written record—is almost as shabby as my personal memory. To take but one key example, the newspapers at the time reported that Franklin County Sheriff Wayne Hutto made some phone calls and located the boys in Louisiana. "I can't figure it out," Hutto is quoted as saying. "If these boys had been in any trouble around here I think I would have known about it."

But Mississippi in 1964 was a police state, meaning simply that the police were complicit with the Klan terrorists, Hutto in this case having helped the Klan search for weapons in the church in Roxie.

We know all these details because the Dee-Moore murder case was in fact solved by the FBI within months of the discovery of the bodies. The FBI had a paid informant in the Klan, a man to whom the killers told the whole story of what happened on May 2, 1964.

This is why in late October of that year the FBI was able to send navy divers into the muddy waters around Parker's Island and find the skeletal remains of the victims, along with the Jeep engine block. Charles Moore's skull was found—identified because he had lost some teeth playing football. Henry Dee's skull has never been found.

• • •

At the Neshoba County Fair in Philadelphia, Mississippi, the town where Goodman, Schwerner, and Chaney were murdered, Ronald Reagan kicked off his 1980 presidential campaign by telling a cheering crowd, "I believe in states' rights."

Once a trauma has been properly buried, you can call it to mind but you do not have to.

"The struggle of man against power is the struggle of memory against forgetting," writes Milan Kundera. But as with all large abstractions, the assertion can be inverted. The Republican Party's "Southern strategy" made the memory of racial difference its tool and when it comes to racial or ethnic differences, the struggle "of man against power" is the struggle of forgetting against memory.

• • •

They say that one way to lay a traumatic memory to rest is to create a particular kind of symbol: a grave marker. Once a grave has been marked, you can visit it but you do not have to. Once a trauma has been properly buried, you can call it to mind but you do not have to. It's available but not intrusive, not haunting.

"The first symbol in which we recognize humanity . . . is the burial," writes Jacques Lacan. "It is man who invented the sepulcher . . . One cannot finish off someone who is a man as if he were a dog . . . [His] register of being . . . has to be preserved by funeral rites."

This is from Lacan's seminar on *Antigone*, a play in which we find no proper burial. *Antigone* ends with three suicides, and suicide can be thought of as an attempt to name through action what ought to be named through inscription. Lacan calls naming through inscription "the second death." "The symbol . . . [is] the killing of the thing," he writes, drawing on Hegel, whose idea was that conceptual understanding is a kind of erasure of the particular.

Take a living dog that runs and barks and eats and shits. As soon as that dog passes into the word *dog*, its particular embodiment disappears: the word *dog* doesn't run and bark and so forth.

Let us put this in terms of trauma. A very particular, horrifying thing happens to someone—as happened to the families of Dee and Moore. How to recover from (or at least work with) such horror? The advice is to erase the particular by putting it into symbols. If the story cannot be fully told, then the trauma persists. Time stops. Twenty years later, the dead still appear in dreams.

The grave marker is the symbol that makes it clear that whatever has happened need not live forever. The symbol lives on but the real, once properly inscribed, is temporal and can be buried.

Forgetting is the erasing angel that murders particularity so that concepts can be born, so that time can flow again.

Forgetting is the erasing angel that murders particularity so that concepts can be born, so that time can flow again.

. . .

In January 1965 the murder charges against James Ford Seale and Charles Marcus Edwards were dismissed, and law enforcement at every level—county, state, and federal—abandoned the case. Several journalists showed some interest in it during the 1990s, but nothing began to move until the summer of 2005, when Canadian filmmaker David Ridgen got in touch with Charles's older brother, Thomas Moore.

Thomas Moore is the central character in the rest of this tale.

He was in the army when his brother was killed and though he came home for the funeral, his mother told him that there was nothing he could do, that he had to forget about it and go on with his life. The army sent him to Vietnam, and he later served in the first Gulf War. He retired to Colorado Springs in the 1990s. During all his years in the military, Moore had nightmares about his brother's death. He would hear Charles calling out for help, asking "Why?" The killing left him feeling trapped, he has said, "chained by pain, guilt, hate, and shame."

Ridgen persuaded Moore to go back to Mississippi and work on the case. Within weeks they had remarkable success: they found James Ford Seale (who had been reported dead) and they found what were supposedly lost FBI files. Soon they confronted Seale's conspirator, Charles Marcus Edwards, directly, approaching him one morning as he and his wife came to open the church where he was a deacon.

Left to Right: James Ford Seale and Charles Marcus Edwards

In Ridgen's film, *Mississippi Cold Case*, we see Moore hand Edwards a manila envelope of FBI files and we hear him ask Edwards why the files contain his name. Edwards protests, "I'm not on the FBI report" (he had in fact never seen the files). "I did not kill your brother," he says. "The FBI dropped all this case and you know that. They dropped the case because there wasn't any evidence. I've never been on that Mississippi River in my life," he says, shooing Moore and Ridgen away. "You all get off this church ground and quit stirring up trouble here on the church."

Not long after this encounter, Moore and Ridgen persuaded a US Attorney in Jackson to give Edwards immunity in exchange for his testimony and to indict Seale for conspiracy in the murders. In 2007 Seale was convicted and sent to jail, where he died four years later.

• • •

This past summer I went back to Mississippi. On May 2, 2014—fifty years to the day after the kidnapping, beating, and murders of Charles Moore and Henry Dee—Moore, Ridgen, and I visited the site in the Homochitto National Forest where the boys had been tied to a tree and whipped until one of them invented the story about guns hidden in a nearby church. Two sticks leaning against a tall yellow pine marked the spot of the beating. I dropped a digital recorder into my shirt pocket and Moore and I, standing on the dirt road amid the filtered sunlight and the bugs, began to talk.

What was of most interest to me was not Seale's conviction—that was simple justice—but something surprising that happened at the trial: Edwards asked the families to forgive him for his part in the crime. In her book *The Human Condition*,

Hannah Arendt addresses "the predicament of irreversibility," our "being unable to undo what [we have] done" such that the deeds of the past hang over every new generation. "Forgiving," she writes, offers a "possible redemption from the predicament of irreversibility."

I knew in general what had happened at the Seale trial, but I was glad to hear Moore tell it in his own words:

> The first day of court . . . it was about four o'clock . . . and he [Edwards] said, "Can I address the court?" and the judge says, "Well, let me dismiss the jury"—and I was sitting right on the front seat—he was still in the witness box and Thelma [Collins, Henry Dee's sister] was sitting next to me . . . and he, looking right at me, he asked me, he said, "Mr. Moore and Mrs. Collins," he said, "I wants to apologize for what I was involved in forty-one years ago, in the killing of your brother." And he said, "I ask your forgiveness." Those were the words. And that was it.

> Everybody's mouth was just, *whup!* an' I said, "Holy shit."

> So then, I had several family members there . . . and I went to each one and I said, "What do you think?" They said, "That's up to you. You got to deal with it." I said, well, I was readin' the Bible—'cause I was brought up in Sunday school—and I read where

it said, "How many times do I forgive my brother? Shall I forgive my brother seven times? No, seventy times seven." And then I said, "I'm goin' to forgive him and give him a handshake." So we did, next morning.

Moore's decision to forgive Edwards would have been hard to predict. The US Army had trained Moore as a rifleman, then as a machine gunner, then as a sniper. "You were a dangerous man," I said, and he agreed. In fact, when it became clear that his brother had been killed simply for being black, Moore began to plot revenge against whites in Franklin County. He stockpiled automatic weapons. He imagined climbing the water tower and poisoning the town water supply. Only when his mother found out what he was up to, and told him not to do it, did he forbear.

Standing with Moore on that dirt road in the forest, I kept circling this change of heart, wondering how he had moved from being a trained, revenge-seeking rifleman to being a man willing to forgive. He kept putting off a direct answer, or so it seemed until I realized he was building it up slowly, for it had many parts.

The first had to do with finding out what had actually happened. In 2005, when Ridgen approached him about filming, Moore asked, "What's in this for me?" and Ridgen replied, "Maybe a little truth." Until that time, Moore had not actually known how his brother had been killed or by whom.

In short, in describing his change of heart, Moore began by speaking of truth and justice (or, as he said to me, "some justice"—of the many men involved in the murders, only one went to jail). It was especially the Seale indictment, and the fact that Moore himself was instrumental in securing it, he said, that had "redeemed [him] from being angry."

"Forgiving," writes Arendt, "is the only reaction which does not merely re-act but acts anew and unexpectedly." That day in the courthouse, Moore and Edwards had quoted back and forth to each other the Christian Gospel about forgiveness, a common language known to both men but belonging to neither, what a psychiatrist friend of mine calls "the third," that is, a thing that allows two people to step beyond themselves into something other than opposition.

Nor was that the end of it. After Seale's conviction, Moore "continued to read about forgiveness":

Moore: Research, research, research. Get an understanding. And I read this thing where it said it was a three-part process. Two of them you have a whole lot to do with—you got to want to do it . . . —it talks about what you holding in—Who is it really hurting? And then I said, then the third part must be the Holy Spirit, to come in and take the place of all that violent mind. And of course I was in the church then; I

was moving, I was moving. Marcus [Edwards] opened the door, gave me the key. Now a lot of people have asked me, "Do you think Marcus was serious?" I don't know. And I really don't care. I really don't care whether he was trying to make himself look good. I don't care. I don't know. He dangled some keys in front of me, and I took 'em. And I let myself out of my own suffering, my poor prison. And I was able to let it go . . . and let my brother lie, just settle down. I think my brother's got peace.

Hyde: But do you still dream about your brother?

> "Forgiving," writes Arendt, "is the only reaction which does not merely re-act but acts anew and unexpectedly."

Moore: No. No, no, no, no. No, I look at the work that I'm doing in church, in the community. I look at it as my brother and my mom, they lookin' down on me and sayin', "He doin' some good stuff." So, as horrible and as brutal as it was, I have come—through the spiritual life—to accept the fact that this was something that I was destined to do, and go *through* in my life in order to be who I am today.

· · ·

In the Erechtheum on the Acropolis in Athens there once stood, says Plutarch, an altar to *Lêthê*, to Forgetfulness, meant to remind Athenians to forget a mythic dispute between Poseidon and Athena. Each god had sought to win the city's favor with a gift, Poseidon offering a spring of salty water and Athena—the winner—an olive tree. Defeated, Poseidon did not begrudge the loss but took it, says Plutarch, with "an easy-going absence of resentment." The altar to Forgetfulness tells the city that the foundational divine discord is to be left to the past, not brought forward.

. . .

James Ford Seale was convicted in 2007. Three years later Thomas Moore returned to Mississippi, this time to seek out Charles Marcus Edwards to see if it was possible to move beyond truth and justice to something closer to true reconciliation. David Ridgen filmed their encounter. After some preliminary greetings, the two men sit on Edwards's porch swing and Moore initiates the conversation:

Moore: I don't know how you feel about it but when you stood up in church, I mean stood up in the court and asked for forgiveness, that gave me *an avenue*.

Edwards: Yeah, right.

Moore: Man, I hated you, dude. I'm gonna tell you right off, I said "I'm gonna get him," you know, and I didn't even know you.

Edwards: You know, when I did that, being in the church, and I'd prayed about that a lot of times, for forgiveness, you know. And it lifted a burden off of me, yes sir, it lifted a burden off of me. That was a black mark in my life, I can't tell you. I'm sorry for it to this day. I was sincere when I asked you and Miss Dee to forgive me too, you know. I didn't deny being a member of the Klan. I didn't deny that.

Ridgen [*voice-over*]: Soon the conversation turns to the beating itself.

Edwards: I reckon you could say Curtis [Dunn] and myself we did the little strapping that went on. James Seale says I—he held a gun on these guys . . .

Moore: I try to think that the shock and that they was on the, uh, how bad they were beaten up I don't know, but just the fact that, I know . . .

Edwards: They got a pretty good whuppin' but I—they was nowhere near dead nor nothing like that, I mean, they were good and alive when

> The altar to Forgetfulness tells the city that the foundational divine discord is to be left to the past, not brought forward.

they left [*unintelligible*] and took them back down to Mr. Seale's place down there before those other people came out there.

Moore: Did you ever think about: "What if that had happened to *my* son?"

Edwards: Well sure I did. And I wondered, you know, I wondered, I had four boys, and I wondered, and I said, "What if some of them people might retaliate and take one of my sons," you know, and I wondered about that.

Ridgen [*voice-over*]: After two hours, and the conversation becoming ever more personal, the coffee comes out.

We see Edwards bringing coffee mugs from his kitchen, then he and Moore stand by Moore's car.

Moore: What does this talking that you and I are doing do for you today?

Edwards: Well, let you know that we can be friends.

Moore [*nods*]: Yeah.

The scene switches back to the men sitting on the porch swing. Moore recalls the time he approached Edwards at his church.

Moore: We didn't come to see you until 2006 because I'm gonna tell you why. I'm gonna tell you why: because

I didn't have the *nerve* to come talk to you. So I, me and David rode by here a couple of times and I said, "No, I'm not goin' in there." That was in 2005.

Edwards: I tell you what, and I look back at the day that you all came to church up there and [*unintelligible*] I thought about it a thousand times since then: "Why didn't I just ask them people to come on in the church with me?"

Moore: What time is your church service on Sunday? The service.

Edwards: The service is at eleven o'clock. [*pauses*] If you want to come, you come.

Moore: I think—you and I, sittin' up in church, is going to be a testimony for our people.

Edwards [*nods*]: Okay.

The men go into the garden to pick peaches and tomatoes. They shake hands by the car.

Moore: We'll be seeing you, fellah.

Edwards [*nodding*]: Uh-huh.

Moore: I remember the words you said, "You all get off of here now, go home." All right, sir, we'll see you Sunday.

In Memory of
Henry Hezekiah Dee
&
Charles Eddie Moore

Kidnaped by the Ku Klux Klan near this spot on May 2, 1964.
Dee and Moore were later beaten,
attached to iron weights, and drowned
in the old Mississippi River.
Their partial remains
were first discovered
on July 12, & 13, 1964.

Moore and Ridgen drive away, Moore shaking his head in disbelief.

Moore: I'm damn near speechless, myself. Five years ago, we talkin' this kind of shit, you crazy as hell. [*smiling*] And instead I'm telling the man that "I planned to kill you. I plotted." And the biggest thing is that he invited us to his church. I didn't expect that. I didn't expect him to say, "You all come on to the church." That's going to be a *story*. God damn it, black and white *do not* attend church together.

. . .

Years before this encounter, at the time of the Seale trial, when Moore forgave Edwards, the two men quoted to each other Jesus's answer when asked how many times a man should be forgiven. Seven times? No, says Jesus, not seven but seventy times seven.

By the time I interviewed Moore I had read Matthew 18:2–6, where this counsel is found. Jesus has a child brought before him and tells the disciples that they should humble themselves "and become like children." Then he says, "Whoever causes one of these little ones . . . to sin, it would be better for him if a great millstone were hung round his neck and he were thrown into the sea."

How would Moore read that line, I wondered. Isn't Jesus saying that some sinners should be put to death rather than be forgiven? Didn't the Klansmen cause one another to sin? Didn't Edwards single out Henry Dee for kidnapping and thus "cause" the murders?

In her meditation on forgiveness, Arendt allows that there are such things as radical evil and unforgiveable crimes. Jesus connects forgiveness and repentance but what exactly is repentance? Arendt points out that the biblical Greek for "repentance" means "change of mind." It isn't enough to say, "I'd like to apologize." What is called for is a conversion and true conversions are rare; one or two in a lifetime would be unusual. What exactly, I wondered, had Charles Marcus Edwards done to show that he had become a different person? In the filmed conversation, he is remarkably passive; Moore does all the work.

And as for reconciliation, isn't what we're seeing an American individualist form—*one* person guilty, *one* person apologizing, *one* person forgiving? What about a legal system that allowed a century of American apartheid, that allowed county, state, and federal law enforcement to ignore two murders for forty years?

I had been thinking about all of this before I met Thomas Moore, and had papers in my pocket with notes to help me fill out my questions. But as we stood

> What is called for is a conversion and true conversions are rare; one or two in a lifetime would be unusual.

talking in the forest where the boys were tortured, my questions seemed out of place, almost rude, thought experiments for some other day.

Instead of pestering Moore about that great millstone, I thanked him for the work he had done. It wasn't my brother who had been killed. I was not the man whose nightmares had been quieted.

. . .

"To study the Buddha Way is to study the self," writes Dogen Zenji, thirteenth-century Japanese Zen master. And "to study the self is to forget the self. To forget the self is to be verified by all things." This last line is a little hard to translate. Some say that forgetting the self is "to be actualized by myriad things"; some say it's "to be enlightened."

In Dogen's original text, the Chinese character for "forget" is made of two elements: the lower half indicates "heart/mind" while the upper half means "to become invisible, perish, lose." The oldest version of this upper part, found on oracle bones dating back three or four thousand years, is a bit of a pictogram: it inserts a vertical line beside the sign for "person" so as to indicate a person hidden behind something and thus invisible.

When something is forgotten, the heart/mind no longer sees it. You could therefore translate Dogen's "self-forgetting" this way: "When we study the self . . . it disappears."

. . .

The story of Thomas Moore's journey from vengeance to forgiveness has two kinds of memory and thus two kinds of forgetting. Some things can be called to mind at will, and some intrude upon the mind no matter what we will. It is one thing to get angry when thinking back on an injury; it is quite another to be invaded by nightmares whenever sleep lowers the threshold of consciousness.

In Greek mythology, the Furies are embodiments of unforgettable grief and rage. Their names are Grievance, Ceaseless, and Blood-Lust. Their names are Grudge, Relentless, and Payback. They clog the fatted present with the undigested past. They harry the sleepless mind, demanding ransom in blood for its release.

There are certain parasitic fungi that invade the brains of tropical ants, making them climb to the top of trees and die there so the fungus can grow from their bodies and widely spread its spores. In the same way, the Unforgettables control their hosts and seed themselves anew. The curse of the House of Atreus descends generation to generation. The story has no closure, each of its bearers being compelled to add another chapter and act it out in the real world.

In the case at hand, the US Army put weapons in Moore's hands and taught him how to kill; add to that his brother's restless, nightmare ghost and before long you have a man plotting to murder white men in Meadville, Mississippi.

Of the many forces that combined to alter and close that plot, three stand out. First there was the truth: in 2005, after forty-one years, Moore got access to the FBI files and knew for the first time what actually happened to his brother. Then there was justice ("some justice"): the government indicted James Ford Seale, a jury in Mississippi convicted him, a federal judge sent him to prison. Only after all of that did forgiveness enter the picture, and forgiveness, as we saw, turned out to be an object of study for Moore: "Research, research, research. Get an understanding."

To enter the work of forgiveness it may not be necessary for the truth to come out and justice to be done, but it helps. It helps because it then becomes easier for the injured man to see the degree to which the wound has become part of his identity, his sense of self. If he is to change he will first of all have to study that self, become intimate with it. That doesn't mean a literal forgetting of the crime but it does mean letting go of the person the crime brought into being. "Why drag about this corpse of your memory?" asks Emerson in one of his great odes to American self-renewal. Said Moore: "As hard and as brutal as it was . . . this was

something that I was destined . . . to go *through* in my life in order to be who I am today." Who he is today is a man who has laid the ghost to rest ("my brother's got peace"), freed himself from servitude to the Unforgettable, and become the agent of his own recollections.

From the point of view of the parasitic fungus, seizing the ant's brain is a wonderful thing. The fungus community endures and spreads. From the point of view of the ant, it's a disaster. In the human community, the spirit of the Unforgettable is useful when it comes to asserting self against other. The desire for revenge can be an expression of basic self-respect and, as legal scholar Martha Minow writes, "vengeance is also the wellspring of a notion of equivalence that animates justice." But revenge without justice too easily descends into unending violence, blacks and whites killing one another year after year as each race claims and defends an identity rooted in *not* being the other.

For those whose goal is an end to conflict, then, better to become intimate with the self that clings to difference. And better to forget about it.

PAUL KIRCHNER

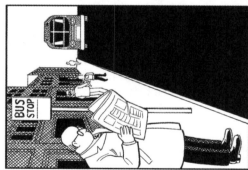

BUS STOP

the bus

PAUL KIRCHNER

the bus

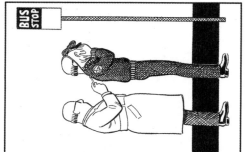

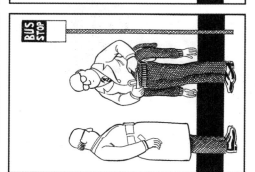

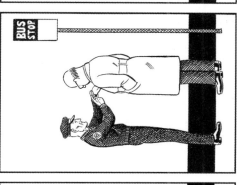

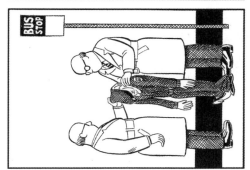

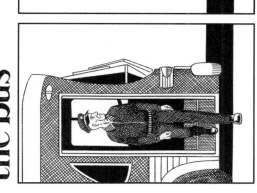
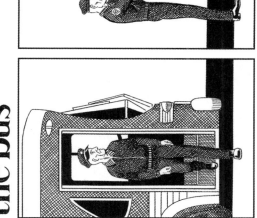

HEAT INDEX

ON BARBARA GRIZZUTI HARRISON'S

Off Center
_____

RACHEL RIEDERER

I read Barbara Grizzuti Harrison's essays for the first time when I was in a creative writing graduate program where I regularly sat through conversations about my class-mates' admiration for Joan Didion. One friend saw Didion on the street and had a quasi-religious experience; another typed and retyped her favorite Didion sentences to internalize the great stylist's spirit. I could never join in the ecstatic reverence, but could also never put my finger on precisely why.

Then I read Harrison's 1980 essay collection *Off Center*. Like Didion, Harrison was writing personal essays and cultural criticism in the seventies, eighties, and nineties. Harrison is often remembered primarily as Didion's detractor—her *New York Times* obituary mentions that she once called Didion a "neurasthenic Cher." This epithet comes from her scathing takedown of Didion, "Joan Didion: Only Disconnect," originally published in the *Nation* in 1979. "My charity does not naturally extend itself to someone whose lavender love seats match exactly the potted orchids on her mantel," writes the ever class-conscious Harrison, who grew up in Queens. But the essay is not a lumpy person's attack on elegance. Instead, it rails against the idea that style (in prose) is argument, the idea that style (in life) is everything. Harrison critiques Didion's 1966 essay "Some Dreamers of the Golden Dream," in which Didion reports on the case of Lucille Maxwell Miller, a California woman found guilty of killing her husband by setting him on fire. "Lucille Maxwell is convicted—by Didion—of wearing polyester and Capris, of living in a house with a snack bar and a travertine entry, of speaking in clichés . . . of frequenting the Kapu-Kai Restaurant-Bar and Coffee Shop, and of never having eaten an artichoke." Didion convicts Miller of being tacky. Harrison convicts Didion of being shallow: "It isn't Didion's sense of morality that has suffered a blow," Harrison writes, after describing the burnt body of Miller's husband, "it's her sense of style." At a moment when I was trying to figure out my own writing voice, I found Harrison's philosophy liberating: a writerly presence could—should!—be made not just from aesthetics but also from morals.

I returned to this essay recently, reminded of it by the new Céline ad that features an elegant eighty-year-old Didion sporting a silver bob and giant black sunglasses. I was shocked, this time, by how very mean the essay seems. The dismantling of Didion's style is, for a writer, the stuff of nightmares: Harrison notices several categories of sentences that Didion uses, names them, lists examples of each. Her tone oscillates only between fierce and mocking. The clarity of the analysis is obvious, but so is its spite.

Harrison's analytical mind is so razor-edged, her ability to connect details with their meanings so precise, that it seems almost unfair for an individual person to be the object of her gaze. More often, and to better effect, her eagle eye is trained not on a person but on an institution. In these situations her scrutiny feels not just appropriate, but essential. In her 1976 essay "Invasion of the Mind-Stealers," Harrison chronicles a weekend est (Erhard Seminars Training) conference. Est taught adherents that they could create their own experiences and "disappear" the obstacles in their lives. Harrison wrote the piece at a moment when est was attracting thousands of trainees, but she, predictably, is having none of it. After her first day of training she asks a classmate: "Does a napalmed baby 'cause his own experience'?" When she sees that the weekend training requires her to sign a form agreeing to keep the material confidential, she tells an est trainer that she needs to call her agent and editor before signing. It is Friday afternoon, though, and a holiday weekend, so she doubts that they will be in their offices. The est trainer suggests that if she calls with the intention of finding them at their desks, then at their desks they shall be. "Can she be suggesting that I can cause them to be in? That my thoughts are a magic carpet that will transport them from East Hampton to midtown Manhattan?" This is funny, but it's the next line that perfectly captures Harrison's worldview: "I would find that kind of power abhorrent."

Her essays are at their best when she turns her analysis inward, and Harrison is as unsparing with herself as she ever was with Didion. In "Growing Up Apocalyptic," published in 1975, she recounts her childhood conversion to "a fierce messianic sect"—she and her mother became Jehovah's Witnesses when she was nine. She captures both the religion's pernicious influence on her adolescence and her own complicity in the process: "I wished to be eaten up alive; and my wish was granted." Echoes of Harrison's messianic childhood can be found throughout her writing. She frequently uses the categories *good* and *evil*, applying them to politics and popular culture in a way that seems not just dated but archaic.

Harrison moved to Bethel, the Jehovah's Witnesses' organizational headquarters, at age nineteen. For three years she lived there, one of twelve women who served as housekeepers for the two hundred and fifty male church leaders. When she was promoted from making beds and cleaning bathrooms to proofreading the *Watchtower* publications, a church elder reminded her that the new position would come with temptations to pride—she must remember to defer to the brothers even as she corrected them. "There were days when I felt literally as if my eternal destiny hung upon a comma: if the brother with whom I worked decided a comma should go out where I wanted to put one in, I prayed to Jehovah to forgive me for that presumptuous comma," she recalls. "I denied and denied—commas, split infinitives, my sexuality, my intelligence, my femaleness, my yearning to be part of the world." At age twenty-two she left Bethel, and the Jehovah's Witness organization, and embraced all the elements—grammatical and personal—that she had been denying herself.

Reading Harrison in 2015 is jarring. Her unapologetic morality feels strange and at the same time is a tonic for pervasive irony. At a cultural moment when there's perennial discussion about whether negative book reviews should ever be published, yet Internet comments spew anonymous vitriol every second of the day, her willingness to offer harsh criticism while maintaining eye contact seems almost alien. Her insistence that style not be mistaken for substance is more important than ever, as our lives become more and more curated and we internalize the idea of the personal brand. Harrison died in 2002—how I wish we had just one essay from her about this new marketing of the self. Her way of looking at the world is deeply unfashionable. That's part of what makes it indispensable.

ON H.D.'S

Bid Me to Live

JONATHAN RUSSELL CLARK

Fall, 1912. The poet Hilda Doolittle and Ezra Pound are at a bun shop by the British Museum. She shows him some poems: "Hermes of the Way," "Acon," and "Orchard." Pound, despite having been briefly engaged to Doolittle in 1907, views her as a student, even using a red pencil to make revisions. After he finishes, he signs "H.D. Imagiste" at the bottom of "Hermes of the Way." Thus begins imagism, a poetic movement focused on clear, concrete language and, appropriately, imagery.

I hate this story. First of all, it's not really a story about H.D. at all, is it? It's a story about Pound—his taste, his acknowledgment, his *approval*. He abbreviates Doolittle's name into a genderless acronym and christens her style. The anecdote wouldn't be so grating, however, if it were not

attached to nearly every introductory bio of H.D., in her books, in encyclopedias, forever rendering her Pound's *imagiste*.

The truth is that Doolittle was much more than an imagist poet, a fact announced to me forcefully when I happened upon her novel, *Bid Me to Live*, in a used-books shop in Wilmington, North Carolina. Though I purchased it as a curiosity, I immediately recognized Doolittle's novel as revelatory. I had believed the narrative that Pound's stamp had created just over a hundred years earlier, that H.D. worked only in images associated with austere lyrics steeped in Greek mythology. How the hell didn't I know that she also wrote intimate, autobiographical fiction?

Though *Bid Me to Live* was not published until 1960, it is undoubtedly a work of modernism. Doolittle composed the novel shortly after the year in which it is set, 1917, smack in the middle of a great sea change in both literature and social hierarchies. As Helen McNeil notes in her introduction, the modernist "pecking order of genius" excluded women "while strong personalities like [D. H.] Lawrence and the huckster-genius Pound flourished." Doolittle, then, had the world against her. Worse still were the opinions of her then-husband, Richard Aldington, author of the following words:

> Whenever a woman goes to write a novel she first chooses herself as heroine . . . If she doesn't do that she sermonizes . . . Adam Bede is an allegorical figure representing George Eliot's

better nature. It is probably due to the pernicious influence of this author that women adopt these evil courses. And her indifference to style is typical . . . women are incapable of the indirect method . . . [they are] writers belonging to the great second class.

In the annals of grossly wrongheaded proclamations, this one's just stunning. Every single thing is wrong here. To begin with, Aldington published these words in *The Egoist* in 1914, as modernism began to show its effect on literature. The period would feature myriad works in which the protagonist is a thinly disguised version of the author. Novelists were moving ever inward, re-creating the rhythm of consciousness through a rigorous reconsideration of the uses of language. Narrative took a backseat to intense self-investigation. Doppelgängers abounded: Proust's Marcel, Hemingway's Nick Adams and Jake Barnes, et al., Joyce's Stephen Dedalus and Leopold Bloom, Faulkner's Yoknapatawpha County. I suppose when men do it, it's art, but when women do it, it's unimaginative.

Secondly, underneath the misogyny is another sinister argument: that roman à clef is somehow lesser than so-called "imagination," as if self-reflection inherently can't aspire to the insight that comes with acts of wholesale invention. This makes it all the more satisfying to read *Bid Me to Live*, in which Doolittle quietly and beautifully contradicts the reprehensibly sexist thesis of her ex-husband.

Doolittle's stand-in in *Bid Me to Live* is Julia Ashton, an American poet living in London. Her marriage is crumbling in the wake of a miscarriage, and the war repeatedly pulls her husband Rafe (Aldington) away from their home. When he does return, he takes up with a mistress, Bella, the upstairs neighbor. Meanwhile, Julia has begun a flirtatious, cerebral correspondence with Frederick, or Rico (or, in life, D. H. Lawrence). The promise of Rico, for Julia, allows a temporary acceptance of Rafe's affair. But in an incredible moment on which the entire novel hinges, Rico comes to London with his German wife, Elsa (Frieda Lawrence), and Julia, hoping to reinvigorate her dormant sexuality, approaches him:

> She got up; as if at a certain signal, she moved toward him; she edged the small chair toward his chair. She sat at his elbow, a child waiting for instruction. Now was the moment to answer his amazing proposal of last night, his "for all eternity." She put out her hand. Her hand touched his sleeve. He shivered, he seemed to move back, move away, like a hurt animal, there was something untamed, even the slight touch of her hand on his sleeve seemed to have annoyed him.

In his letters to Julia, Rico has made his intentions known ("We will go away together where the angels come down to earth," he writes), but here his shiver, his ever-so-brief reluctance, crushes Julia, leaving her vulnerable to the pain of her husband's affair. Fearing that the nosy landlord might discover the tryst, Julia tells Rafe and Bella to sleep in her room, but they immediately and carelessly take it as an opportunity for sex, occupying Julia's bed. Bella adds further injury by complaining to Julia that she "tyrannize[s] [Rafe's] soul" and demands that he choose between them. He chooses Bella. Julia's already collapsing life becomes rubble.

Like Aldington, Rico has strong opinions about how and what a woman can write. He advises Julia: "Stick to the woman-consciousness . . . it is the intuitive woman-mood that matters." And H.D. writes: "But if he can enter, so diabolically, into the feelings of women, why should not she enter into the feelings of man?" Why not, indeed. There isn't anything Julia or Doolittle can rightly do: Doolittle's husband believes that women shouldn't write about themselves, and Rico as Lawrence believes that a woman shouldn't try to write about men. What, then, are they supposed to write?

In the end, Julia travels to Cornwall with the composer Vane (Cecil Gray, with whom Doolittle eventually had a child, Perdita), a man about whom Rico has said to Julia, "You are made for one another." There she experiences a kind of catharsis. The rocks and fields soothe her, and she contemplates Rico, Rafe, Bella, all of it. She writes Rico a letter in which she tells him: "I will never see you again, Rico." But her decision has less to do with Rico's faults than with her continued devotion to him. She *can't* see him again. Rico's rejection caused not hate but more love. "You can write a book about us," she tells him, but she doesn't want Rafe or Bella or Vane to be in it, too. Referring to Rico's gender separation, she concludes: "You can't light fire on an altar unless the altar is there. You are right about man-is-man, woman-is-woman, I am wrong. But it's no good. My work is nothing. But, Rico, I will go on and do it. I will carve my pattern on an altar because I've got to do it." Julia never fully rebukes Rico. I suspect it's because she never believes he deserves it. She continues, to the end, to harbor deep feelings for him. The only satisfaction of her final letter is that she never sends it. Rico doesn't get to read those lines, just as Lawrence never got to read Doolittle's novel. For writers, there can be nothing more pointed than withholding words.

In a way, the novel is like that letter: something unsent. But rather than representing a lost opportunity, to me it's about what we keep for ourselves. This work, these words, they belong to Hilda Doolittle. They do not belong to Richard Aldington, or D. H. Lawrence, or Ezra Pound. Let us hope that history redefines H.D. by these words, *her* words, and erases Pound's stamp, not to replace it with another descriptor like *novelist* or *artist* or even *woman*. "It's all self-portrait," H.D. writes of art, and in *Bid Me to Live* we have a candid, touching, revelatory portrait, formed by her own art, created in her own image.

Eleven Blue Men and Other Narratives of Medical Detection

JESSICA HANDLER

On a September evening in 1934, Roberto Ramirez smelled burning meat in his Manhattan apartment. Looking down, he discovered that his cigarette had burned the flesh on his fingers until they were "cracked and curling and darkly red." He hadn't felt the pain. More innocuously, on April 6, 1942, a man called Herman Sauer "passed through the general clinic of Lenox Hill Hospital, at Seventy-sixth Street and Park Avenue." He had a stomachache, a minor complaint—or so it seemed.

These are fragments of true-life stories from Berton Roueché's 1953 book, *Eleven Blue Men and Other Narratives of Medical Detection*, a collection of the Annals of Medicine pieces he wrote for the *New Yorker*, where he was a staff writer for nearly half a century. Roueché's articles probed weirdly random cases of cyanosis, trichinosis, and gout almost fifty years before the launch of the Diagnosis column in the Sunday *New York Times* or the era of ever-replicating medical-detective TV shows like *CSI* or *Forensic Files*. (In fact, some episodes of the TV medical drama *House* are inspired by *Eleven Blue Men*.) But *Eleven Blue Men* is far from a pulp anachronism or a parade of horror tales. Roueché was too elegant a writer, and the human beings who populate his tales too nuanced, for the stories to be dismissed as lowbrow. And although he wrote in a style I can only call "med-noir," and was given a Raven Award by the Mystery Writers of America, Roueché was more than a mystery or genre writer. He was a narrative nonfiction writer who legitimized the bizarre.

The titular story tells of how a busboy mistakenly fills saltshakers with sodium nitrate in a flophouse cafeteria kitchen, sending eleven elderly derelicts to the hospital with symptoms including retching, diarrhea, and oxygen deprivation: cyanosis, determined from their "sky blue" extremities. Roueché's investigators are the real men and women (mostly men, it being the middle of the last century) of the Bureau of Preventable Diseases, the sanguine name for the New York City Department of Health's division of medical gumshoes: intrepid, cigar-chomping doctors who rely on unflappable nurses, secretaries with solid-gold instincts, and regular Joes who follow their hunches.

In "The Alerting of Mr. Pomerantz," Roueché gives us an exterminator who has "that Stonewall Jackson feeling" as he enters a Queens building searching for mites, sure that the tiny arachnids are the cause of the tenants' mysterious pox. He's right, and working in conjunction with Dr. Robert Huebner of the United States Public Health Service, he contributes to the discovery of rickettsialpox, a rash caused by mite bites. In "The Fog," an eerily calm, transfixing account of a quagmire of industrial smog that killed twenty people in Donora, Pennsylvania, in 1948, Roueché writes of an afternoon "black as a derby hat." In "A Game of Wild Indians," Roueché describes a calm clerk named Beatrice Gamso (can't you just see her legs?), calling her, dryly, "a low-strung woman."

At one time, the weird accounts in *Eleven Blue Men* were required reading for the Centers for Disease Control and Prevention's Epidemic Intelligence Service doctors. These are the epidemiologists dispatched to the sites of outbreaks: think Ebola in Africa and the United States, or airborne toxicity after the 9/11 attacks. That same little blue paperback that was part of CDC field workers' training came into my consciousness in the 1970s, in a brick ranch house two miles from the main campus of the CDC in Atlanta. The book was my father's, something he'd come across at a bookstore or gotten on a friend's recommendation. I was a precocious kid in a house full of sick people, and, like my father, I read *Eleven Blue Men* looking for answers. The book made the illnesses in my home—leukemia, neutropenia, drug addiction, and what was at the time called manic depression—momentarily and calmingly ordinary. The people Roueché portrayed were, by contrast, spectacularly sick, vomiting from the effects of a "voracious endoparasitic worm" in "A Pig from Jersey," or experiencing the "spine-cracking muscular spasm" of tetanus in "A Pinch of Dust."

Doctors showed up at our house at odd hours to take blood or pound backs and chests. Like Roueché's investigators, they smoked cigarettes and posited theories. They were nice people. Lab technicians spun my blood and my sisters' blood and our parents' blood in centrifuges, preparing to examine the jigsaw puzzles of our genes. Throughout all this, I was engrossed in the blue paperback with the line drawing of inky-blue fingers on the cover. Maybe reading Roueché is what made me first conflate writing and medicine.

But doctors, like their patients, are human, and so are fallible. Sometimes they win, and sometimes they lose. They take a few wrong turns before solving somatic riddles. In 1946, eleven men recovered from inadvertent poisoning, and were released back into the streets. Herman Sauer's fatal stomach ailment, trichinosis, was diligently traced to his nibbling of raw pork while cooking for a community feast. Roberto Ramirez? His diagnosis was Hansen's disease, also known as leprosy.

And me? In my house, some of us lived, and some didn't. I looked up from *Eleven Blue Men* and watched people do their best to take care of each other. And then I looked back down, and began to write.

ON AGNES SMEDLEY'S

Daughter of Earth

S. SHANKAR

Agnes Smedley's *Daughter of Earth* was published in 1929, the same year as William Faulkner's *The Sound and the Fury*. Two novels more different would be hard to find—the former is realist fiction of passionate testimony, the latter a modernist classic of formal experimentation. About the deserved fame of Faulkner's novel nothing at all need be said. Unfortunately, the same cannot be assumed for Smedley's amazing novel, which is largely disregarded today.

Daughter of Earth is many things—feminist fiction, proletarian novel, devastating account of American poverty. Smedley herself corresponded to the qualities of her semiautobiographical novel—she was a feminist, a socialist advocate for the working class and the disenfranchised, a scrappy escapee from a life of poverty. Between her birth in 1892 and death in 1950 came an adventurous life of self-education, world travel, and political activism, including in China. During the McCarthy Era she was accused of being a spy but never appeared before the House Un-American Activities Committee, as she left for England. Though she was born in Missouri and died in England, her ashes were buried in Beijing, because of her deep involvement for two decades with Chinese revolutionary movements. Smedley wrote extensively as a journalist, but her novel is surely her crowning achievement as a writer.

Compelling as this life is, *Daughter of Earth* only grows in stature when read without reference to its author's biography, for its literary qualities then become even more evident. Written with a wonderful intimacy born of the first person, the novel belies the routine and ignorant dismissals in some quarters of politically committed literature. Both Smedley's language and development of characters show real literary ambition. Her prose is woven of striking images and precise descriptions; and her characterizations are full of sensitive observations of human behavior. The vivid and emotionally charged opening paragraphs are a good indication of the novel's power. These paragraphs launch the voice of a protagonist at once assured and vulnerable, while simultaneously sketching out the symbolism of sea, sky and especially earth around which the novel is structured:

> Before me stretches a Danish sea.
> Cold, gray, limitless. There is no

horizon. The sea and the gray sky blend and become one. A bird, with outspread wings, takes its way over the depths.

. . .

I write of the earth on which we all, by some strange circumstance, happen to be living. I write of the joys and sorrows of the lowly. Of loneliness. Of pain. And of love.

The sky before me has been as gray as my spirit these days. There is no horizon—as in my life. For thirty years I have lived, and for these years I have drunk from the wells of bitterness. I have loved, and bitterness left me for that hour. But there are times when love itself is bitter.

There you have it—subtle contemplation and beautiful language in a politically committed novel. Commitment the enemy of aesthetic pleasure? Not at all.

The political commitment of *Daughter of Earth* extends to love and marriage, an emotion and an institution Smedley's protagonist Marie Rogers valiantly, if sometimes fruitlessly, resists. The last scenes of the novel are the most convincing and moving exploration of life's impossible choices that I have read in a long time. By the end of the novel Marie, who has thrown herself into a circle of Indian revolutionaries fighting the British Empire from exile in New York, has taken one of these revolutionaries for a lover and then married him. Soon, however, jealousy and misunderstanding intrude to fracture an otherwise idyllic relationship. Marie finds herself desperately mulling love and revolutionary practice, sacrifice and self-determination, the personal and the political. Discarding the tired conventions of bourgeois fiction, Smedley has her heroine choose revolution over love, self-determination over sacrifice, and the political over the personal. It is for this gumption no doubt that Smedley has been relegated to the minor ranks of American literature—never mind that Rogers' choices as Smedley portrays them have the plausibility of life, or that Smedley does not in any way disregard the cost of these choices for her heroine.

Equally powerful scenes occur elsewhere in *Daughter of Earth*, especially the first third of the novel, during which Marie Rogers battles mightily to exit the life of extreme poverty into which she is born. Here we find a closely observed account of the child Marie Rogers' developing consciousness of her difference in class from the rich and the well settled. Smedley gives us harrowing depictions of the mining life, the struggle against hunger, the travails of Marie's mother as a wife, the temptation of prostitution for her aunt. It is only education—attained with great determination and against great odds—that finally allows Marie to leave behind a bare, wretched existence and progress steadily toward an independent life of political action.

Let's be frank: they don't write like this anymore. In contemporary publishing, "literary fiction," ostensibly the home for "serious" writing, has been reduced to formula. Today, literary fiction presents itself as a counterpoint to what is called "genre fiction," but it has become a kind of genre fiction itself. Prose more careful than passionate, rounded and predictably flawed human beings (always the same flaws!), formal hijinks, the exquisite calibration of sincerity with irony: literary fiction unfailingly hashes and rehashes a combination of these and similar features. Again and again it returns directly or else surreptitiously to the well-trodden and safe environs of individual—and also individualist—hopes and fears. It is as if literary fiction is afraid to do what *Daughter of Earth* does—to be passionate, to be committed, to run the risk of sincerity, to advocate for and choose a collective destiny over an individual one. For if it did, might it not become communist or primitive or, worst of all, naïve?

No, we don't write it like *Daughter of Earth* any more. But perhaps we should, if only because our warring, warming, chaotic, fatigued world demands that we do. In a fine foreword to the 1987 Feminist Press reissue of *Daughter of Earth*, Alice Walker called the novel "a precious, priceless book" and declared Smedley "a citizen of the planet." *Daughter of Earth* is a literary triumph fully reflective of the generous conception of citizenship Walker recognizes in Smedley. Now more than ever, our world needs such generosity.

ON ANDRÉ GIDE'S

Paludes

JOHN REED

The literary figures of the mid-twentieth century are simultaneously, paradoxically, cultural heroes and yokel blunderers, stalwart independents and villainous conformists. They are loudmouths about Communism, the greatest political experiment since democracy; they are sometimes proponents and sometimes detractors, and in their arguments they are sometimes perspicacious and sage, and they are sometimes petty and wicked. They are the Russian Revolution, and they are the CIA and the British Secret Service's Congress for Cultural Freedom—which lent massive support to Arthur Koestler, George Orwell, Ernest Hemingway, and Bertrand Russell—with a stated mission of winning a "soft war." They are Ezra Pound and his radio pontifications for the Nazis. They are anti-Semitism and knee-jerk atavism, they are racism and sexism, and they are every other nasty, troll-ish habituation of people-kind. They are also courageous resistance, enormous personal loss, and a Western outlook that expanded, became more inclusive and humane—socially, sexually, racially, and culturally.

But in the beginning, they were children—literary children.

André Gide's early satirical work *Paludes* (1895, in English, *Morasses*) is an allegory of nineteenth-century Paris's cultural world, a quaintly seductive, if frequently silly and petty, vision of the arts. Paul Claudel, in a 1900 letter to Gide, called *Paludes* "the most complete document we have on that curious atmosphere of suffocation and stagnation we breathed from 1885 to 1890."

One hundred years later, readers might see *Paludes* as an ironic treatment of Gide's sexual repression; Gide wrote the novel following a recuperative journey to North Africa, a common remedy for tuberculosis, which evolved into an indulgence of "pagan" delights. *Paludes* is about the Gide who stayed home: a man who suffers from self-imposed subjugation, as a writer and as a homosexual man. The protagonist of *Paludes*, Tityre, is quite content to spend his time writing descriptive passages about a nearby marsh. Tityre is arrogant, insufferable, boring, didactic, and pathetic—so pathetic that he's almost sympathetic. That the literary world around him is even worse speaks to his plight, and thus do we see our analog; Tityre is trying, trying to love his vista of slime and rocks, which is

the suffocating, stagnant Paris of the late nineteenth century. And with the transparency of this analogy, *Paludes* is also a pioneering metanovel—a literary undertaking that takes full swing at a fourth wall that was then still firmly in place.

But perhaps *Paludes* may be regarded most as a young man's unwitting premonition of the old men of the establishment that his generation would become. Gide's epoch was a habitat of impossible contradictions. Everyone was wrong, and everyone was right. To side with the Communists was to condone Stalin; to side with the conservative Western opposition to Communism was to endorse the most obstructive mandate of cultural controls since Rome's annexation of Christianity. Where there was success, there was failure; Communism, as seen by the wide-eyed and optimistic, was just as doomed as democracy, as seen by its own constituency of wide-eyed optimists. Gide's ideologies and writings epitomized the vicissitudes of popular French attitudes, so often xenophobic and self-serving; and at the same time he was staunchly, admirably independent, whatever side or nonside he took. In his later years, the World War II years, he wavered with France, wanting desperately to avoid another global bloodshedding, harboring anti-Semitism, and coming to the understanding, finally, that Hitler was carrying out an unrivaled act of atrocity. In his literary stance on sex, Gide wasn't satisfied with the be-but-don't-say homosexuality of Oscar Wilde and Marcel Proust; yet, personally, Gide was beset by a recurring revulsion for gay sex.

But as much as Gide sought some alternative to the "morasses" of his time, he was uncomfortable with literature as a form of judgment. If Wilde and Proust were hypocritical in their silence, Gide was far more culpable in his vice: underage creatures. Tityre contends with Gide's artistic muddle: while literature may be stifled, ideology is not the answer. In 1934, at a meeting of the Association des Écrivains et Artistes Révolutionnaires, Gide addressed the subject of "Littérature et Revolution" by stating that "literature has no obligation to put itself in service to the Revolution." Gide understood the mistake, the repeated over and again error of the arts in the twentieth—and now the twenty-first—century: "An enslaved literature is a debased literature, however noble and legitimate the cause it serves."

If Gide's half century didn't deliver creative or social utopia, so far, the second half of the twentieth century, plus a few years, has done no better. The pages of *Out* magazine are more haven to luxury advertising than to radical literature. If there is a single cultural truth that has gained momentum for the last one hundred and fifty years, it is that all the advances of the arts can be gathered and deployed in the marketplace. That the creative act is inevitably diminished has come to be regarded as par for the course, as if it is the primary purpose of art to be sacrificed at the altar of stupidity. Politics, a willfully fatuous form of sophistry, is the overlord of the spiritual, the inexplicable, the awesome. That the polarization of political realms has become only more extreme is just another portion of what we have given up; the marketplaces of creative culture are ever prone to the categories and the desires of this economic grotesque, this immersion theater, that we have all condoned. We have become complacent, perhaps even entertained by the spectacle of our own self-disfigurement. And *Paludes*? It's blockbuster, it's cyberpunk. It's literary Paris, nineteenth century, as an apocalyptic swampland. 🜚

GOING UNDER

The nitrous oxide mixed with oxygen
entering the twin nostrils
rubs the mind down.
How I like it, staring at the ceiling
and feeling not one poppy of pain.
The gas tames my reflexes.
My mouth purpling.
Let the needlehead in.
Let the impacted tooth crack,
excavated from the bed of gum
splinter by splinter.
I, lying there and thinking,
So easy to have something taken
like it never grew from me.
A thought
just a thought,
not even my own.

ZUIHITZU

Sunday, and I'm awake with this headache. White clot behind the eyes.

*

Someone once told me, *The future and the past are another binary*. It was midwinter, I had no passport. In my apartment, two mice made a paradise out of a button of peanut butter.

*

What thief came and took off with one of my possible lives? He must've liked symmetry. He saw you and me, and he stole one of yours, too.

*

The cloth of what-is-beginning. And my stranger, myself, hidden in the folds.

*

These days, I've had my fill of Chinatown and its wet markets. Fish entrails. Overcooked chattering. The smell makes me look hard at everything.

*

Let there be no more braiding of words. I want a spare mouth.

*

My father taught me that wherever you are, always be looking for a way out: this opening or that one. Or a question. Sharp enough to slice a hole for you to slip through.

*

Dandruff of the pear tree. Hard to believe another half year has dropped, wooden bead on an abacus.

*

Could it be that the life we want to live is always two steps behind us? Nights when you were already in bed, peeling off strips of dreamspeak.

*

What can pass through sleep? Every morning, I reach my way into a self. But who's leaving them out for me?

*

At four, I loved eating powdered milk straight from the canister. There wasn't money for real milk. Seven hundred years ago, Zhang Yang-hao wrote, *All my life seems like yesterday morning.*

NEW VOICE FICTION

Pink Lotion

Sarah Elaine Smith

I had my instructions on a piece of paper folded in my lap, but I was so nervous in smoothing it against my thigh that I brushed it to the floor by the pedals and had to pull over in a mini-mall plaza to find it and read it again. I was taking a newcomer, Nadine, to an AA meeting. My sponsor thought it would be good for me to do more service work. Service work is what they call it when you do something nobody wants to do, like washing coffee cups or picking up all the cigarette butts in the church parking lot after a meeting. Like any other part of the program, service is suggested in the way you might suggest that a child not bash its head open on a bannister.

My sponsor, Sheila, was six feet tall and had worked as a machinist at the Kyowa America plant for ten years as a drunk and then seventeen more as a sober person. She smoked Marlboro Menthol Milds and kept her nails painted in horrible tropical colors and wanted, I was sure, to kick my ass until serenity somehow appeared to take me away on the wind. Her laugh sounded just like somebody had sent a ratchet clattering down a flight of stairs. Every day I called her at 7:15 AM and told her my troubles. My troubles usually made her laugh.

Nadine, the newcomer, was blind. According to my sponsor, she had passed out in front of the Rock Lick Tavern, facedown in a snowbank, and was not found until much later when a tanker rolled his truck on the hairpin out by Cameron High School and shut down Route 250 in both directions, requiring a crew of recovery vehicles. The driver was gone from the site, and state police canvassed out to the Rock Lick and into Ryerson, where he might have gone on foot for help. And there was Nadine, asleep in the snow. She had been thrown out after getting in a fight with her husband and didn't even make it to her car in the parking lot. As far as I knew, they still hadn't found the driver. It all seemed very suspicious to me. I hadn't been there for a few months, but I knew the people who drank at the Rock Lick. I didn't believe they could let something like that happen to a person.

Nadine had cirrhosis and diabetes and lived in an old folks home off I-79, past the prison, where Waynesburg started looking like any other suburban net of sodium lamps and stores. The orange light made it feel like I was in a large room instead of the outdoors. Where I lived, out in the sticks, it was pure dark like the inside of a lung.

Dedlyn Glen and Apartments announced itself on a gold-lettered brick retaining wall like that of a liberal arts college. I was to take a slight turn off its cul-de-sac and park by the kitchen dumpsters and enter the security code on the pad by the rear door. Nadine would be waiting for me in a chair just through the kitchen, which would be empty at that hour.

I sat in my car and cut the headlights. I could see into the dining room, brightly lit.

He asked me what the fuck I was doing. What the fuck was I doing?

The furniture was particleboard and vinyl like at a Sizzler or a Shoney's, but the room was empty. I liked the warm windows of places seen from outside in the dark, but this was like looking into an abandoned airport. I had left early to give myself enough time to find the home. When I found it, I still had half an hour to blow, so I drove in lazy angles over the empty parking lot.

Newly sober, I spent an awful lot of time in my car. It was a place I had previously occupied only in attitudes of panic and fear. Driving it with clean spit ringing all through me, I could imagine myself being useful someday. I was starting to recognize the names of the radio DJs, their architectures of emotion and self-made nicknames. I often smoked an extra cigarette in the car while waiting for a meeting to start. I had a whole living room in the backseat.

I also chewed gum, ate mints, and drank coffee. Earlier, I had been banging around the kitchen, opening cabinets, looking for something. My boyfriend, Baird, was drinking a beer in the living room and smoking and reading a book hung over his face on a belt strung between the record player and the armchair. He asked me what the fuck I was doing. What the fuck was I doing? I was looking for something I could ingest that would carve out a little pit in time where I could spend the next hour not thinking about the pit, the hour, my life. "I'm looking for my magic beans,"

I said to Baird. "You seen them around?" I found cans of chili and Jell-O boxes and a frozen piecrust furred with frost. There were four Miller Genuine Draft tallboys in the back of the bottom shelf of the refrigerator behind a collection of empty hot sauce bottles, and a half-empty pint of Ten High on its side in the boot pile by the back door. I did not dare look at or touch them, except with my thoughts. I baked the naked piecrust and ate it with salt and hot sauce. It tasted like air-conditioning. Baird was reading *Our Lady of the Flowers*.

Glen and Apartments. I'd pick glen over apartments if I had the choice.

At five of seven, I drove again to the back door and cut the engine. The entry code was 1-2-3-4-5-*, of course, so simple I probably didn't need to record it in shaky ballpoint numerals, as I had done. I had never met Nadine. Inside was a bright emptiness like you see in horror films, the establishing shot before the evil one comes. The dining room was vacant except for stuffed bears and crepe Easter decorations. One deflated bunny hung from its pink plastic ears in an attitude of despair and complaint.

> **Regarding substances, I had been a purist. It was something Baird liked about me. Coffee, cigarettes, whiskey.**

Nadine wore sunglasses, a trench coat, long pants, tall boots, and white gloves. She had a scarf tied around her head and a Chicago Bulls '92 ball cap clamped on top of it. I had seen this look before, I felt, in deposed rulers of unstable nations trying to hide in plain sight. I mean, I had seen it in cartoons. She turned toward the sound of my footfalls.

"Hi, Nadine. It's Shawna. I'm here to take you to the Friday meeting?"

"Something stinks."

"That's me, probably. I was smoking in the car."

"I mean, *really stinks*."

"Okay," I said. "Ha ha." What I could see of her face reminded me, somehow, of margarine.

"Are you one of those girls from the college?"

"Not anymore," I said. "I guess I don't know what you're asking."

"They come here and read to me, if you can believe it."

"That sounds nice."

"The Bible, the Bible, the Bible," she said. "Is the Bible nice? Do you like the Bible?"

"Not really."

"Well, I told *her*. I'm from New York. But anyway."

"We should go."

She held her hand forward in the air. It seemed she expected me to put something in it, a dove or basketball or bowl of fruit salad. A handshake. Her jaw hung down a little. I extended my hand, and she stood and felt her way to my elbow. Her cane had been folded in her lap, its joints held together with elastic. It snapped into shape, the antenna of a curious underwater thing. Walking, it wavered ahead of her. She was not good at using it yet. I didn't hate her anymore. Like an idiot or a mother I told her all of the things that were happening around us. *Here's the door. Let's turn to the right a little. Here's the door. It's cold. It's night.*

One thing I found really funny was how all my friends had despaired of finding coke in Greene County. *It's just impossible*, they said. Baird drove all the way to Baltimore to meet the friend of a dealer he knew from when they were SigEp brothers. He had pooled money with some of the other regulars at the Rock Lick. It was a big deal, hero time. Everybody bought him drinks and gave highway advice. He was doing for us what we could not do, was the way the feeling went. He came around the bar for a boost on his way out of town. He had already stocked the passenger seat with bags of Spanish peanuts and hot fries. He brought a copy of *Lonesome Dove* for if he got bored. So elaborate were the preparations that I was shocked when he came back eight hours later like nothing had happened and put the stuff on the bar. It was in a little Yankee Candle gift bag. A cut on his brow let a slug of blood out occasionally. He said it was from "doing pushups." I could not figure what this meant. But by then, of course, I could only see by the light of the lantern that swung out from my forehead.

As I had learned in AA meetings, it was no hardship to find coke, or ketamine or hydromorphone or anything else, in Greene County. Baird and his friends merely lacked *initiative*. Coke came up so regularly in meetings that after a few months I knew all the relevant corners and motor courts, and how much and what to say, which were not things I had ever known before. Regarding substances, I had been a purist. It was something Baird liked about me. Coffee, cigarettes, whiskey. And beer, but only if it was four in the morning and nothing else was left, or if I felt a tremor go through my hands the next day, or if I was watching baseball on one of those long afternoons with the sprawl of childhood inside it.

But Baird's journey was exciting, and bar regulars lived for invented holidays and temporary enthusiasms. I loved bar Christmas much more than the real thing. Glenda brought *halupki* in vast aluminum dishes and slab pies from the supermarket. Everybody came in wearing new clothes, and with new money.

There was briefly a craze at the Rock Lick for a horrible drink called the Samurai Comfort. It was Southern Comfort and cheap sake, the kind that turns your nasal membranes to paper as you hover over the glass. Dooley's poor try-hard of a son-in-law had given him a Sake Taste Adventure gift set from Sam's Club for Christmas, which he swiftly donated to the tavern for R & D purposes. Glenda wrote "Samurai Comforts" up on the specials board as a joke—seventy-five cents, buy one get one. We drank them without comment whenever we ran out of money. I talked myself into liking them for this reason alone. Dooley said they gave him a little window of second sight in which he saw whatever his estranged wife was looking at that very second. *I see a swimming pool in the desert*, he said. *I see a coyote turning in circles.* She had left him for a soil scientist who lived in Palos Verdes, California, so who was I to besmirch this vision? When the Sake Taste Adventure set ran out, Glenda made a special trip to Wheeling to buy more, but the joke was over. Nobody would touch them but me. They could only be enjoyed as a boon or an accident. I bought the rest of the sake from her at cost and brought it home to drink on my own, a secret even from Baird.

When I lost my job at the tax assessor-collector's office, Dooley boosted us for a few months and got Baird hired on at a contracting company. When I thought I was pregnant, Theresa bought me shot after shot of Johnnie Walker poured up to the lip so we could good and poison that baby right out of living in my body, and then went with me to the clinic the next day. But there was no baby. It was just a lapse in my cycle. Theresa bought me more shots to celebrate.

And when my mother died, I stole the urn from my aunt's house and brought it to the Rock Lick. Glenda let me play my Hoyt Axton song on the jukebox eleven times consecutively before she unplugged it—*Sorry, hon*—and sat with me and Baird. It was August. The ironweed was up all along the road and the leaves were exhausted from being so unendingly green and dark all summer. I drank until my face hurt.

This went on about an hour until Dooley had had enough. He racked the pool table and plugged the jukebox back in.

"Hey," I said. "Hey, hey, hey, hey. What the fuck."

"I'm sorry, Shawna. I am really sorry," he said. "But come on."

"I'm an orphan. I'm an orphan! I don't have a mother."

"You sure do. She's just dead is all."

"Christ, Dooley," Baird said. "Leave it."

"Get her home, bud. This is a happy place."

"Fuck you, Dooley. Fuck you. God," I said.

"Come on, babe." Baird swept the hair back from my shoulder and put an arm around my waist.

"No. You just wanna put me away so you can come back and fuck Glenda."

"Whoa," Baird said.

"Yeah, I see you, asshole. I see you."

Baird said I passed out as soon as he put me in the car, but while he was pulling around off the gravel shoulder I opened the door and fell out spinning. I got up and walked back in the bar. By the time he ran in Dooley had me by the wrists and I was trying to worm my body to get purchase and swing at him. The black eye I had after could have been from anything. It was probably just from rolling in the parking lot, Baird said, as he felt Dooley was my true friend and would not hit me. I remember none of it, of course. I had to wear heavy eye shadow for the next week, and thick, cool makeup to hide the bruise on my jaw. It got to be a joke, so that if ever I walked in looking dolled up for some reason, Dooley would first cower with his hands over his head and then ask me who died.

But there was no baby. It was just a lapse in my cycle. Theresa bought me more shots to celebrate.

I opened the car door for Nadine and she swung her legs around but did not want to get out. The ground skimmed just out of reach from her boots where they kicked, looking for it. Her face twisted with effort. She touched the edge of her tongue to her top lip. I would hate being blind. I like to know just what my face is doing.

"Just scoot forward some," I said. "You'll find it."

"I know that."

"Can I take your purse?"

"Calm down. I got it." It would have been so much easier to just pick her up and fireman-carry her into the meeting. She raised herself up and held out her hand again. I put my elbow in it and led her up the ramp to the clubhouse. Other people moved silently around us. When she heard the whiff of their coats going by, Nadine asked me who's that. *Who's that, hum.* Well, I didn't know. I was new myself, only a little less new than Nadine, and while I had seen so many of the people over and over, their names sailed away from me just as she asked. I knew the smelly guts of them, though. Once, a woman shared about how she got so tired at the end of her drinking that she could not be troubled to do laundry. She had a washer in her basement, but hauling down there with a hamper and all was just, she felt, too much to ask of her. And besides that, stairs had become increasingly challenging. She was bruised all over the shins. So she washed her underwear for a whole year by laying them over the drain while she showered, thinking the shampoo suds would clean them. At the time, she felt very proud of figuring out this trick, and she kept it up even though the wet underwear left big spots of water on her clothes like she had peed herself. This made so much sense to me that I had to touch my mouth while she was talking to make sure I was not talking also, that we were not in fact chanting this depraved thing together. But I didn't know her name.

Sometimes new people really want to air out how much they hate their lives.

I got our coffees and pulled the coat from Nadine's shoulders. She let it hang down around her like it was a rind she had just split and climbed out of. She insisted on holding her purse in her lap. The cane collapsed when you clicked a button on the handle. It had a spring inside it like an umbrella, and I clicked and unclicked it a few times to watch it snap straight.

"This is cool," I said.

"Huh?" Nadine said.

"Your cane. It's like, automatic."

"I do not for Christ know what you are talking about."

"The button," I said. I could not think of another thing to say about it. The wet underwear woman sat at the head of the table and rang the bell by flicking a thumbnail against it, and our voices fell away. She said her name was Wendy, and she was an alcoholic. She was pretty and familiar, like a watercolor painting next to an elevator.

As the usual readings and announcements went on, I lost my edges. This happened pretty often when I was still putting days together. I could see a pulse coming from the overheads, light and rapid like a small animal's rocketing heart. If the others saw this, too, they were much better than I was at hiding it. Molecules of shadow crawled through the low-pile industrial carpet and scattered when I tried to look at them directly.

A man in coveralls was saying how good it felt to have clean blood and how he didn't have to understand it to get on his knees—AM, PM—to say those please and thank-you words and how after that the gifts were given. There was the gift of waking up in the morning and the gift of a truck that would start in the cold and the gift of having a door you could lock behind you at the end of the day.

When Dooley came in, we were already a third of the way around the room. The only empty chair was next to Nadine. She pulled herself up and sniffed as he seated himself. Dooley had a bottle of Gatorade that he passed from hand to hand. When he tried to hold it up to his mouth, it shook and a little went down his chin, so he put it down and punched into his thighs and knitted his fingers together. He smelled medical. I stole looks at his face because I kept forgetting what it looked like, but it was him in the dark mirror the window made. It was the same configuration as when the two of us sat, an empty stool between us, looking into the mirror behind the bar at the Rock Lick. The thing had veins of gold running through it. An old dark dust of tarnish burned in places like clouds of flies or bad thinking or rain that hung unmoving over our shoulders. He caught my glance and pinched off a meager smile for me. When it came his turn to talk, the fumes sank off him in drafts.

"Name Dooley. I'm, I don't know. I guess I'm an alcoholic. Never been to one of these before."

"Hi, Dooley," we all said together. One of the oldtimers started a phone list for him on the back of a trifold meeting schedule and another brought him a cup of coffee. I could feel Dooley's eyes on me but I refused to turn my head. We waited for him to say more. Sometimes new people really want to air out how much they hate their lives.

"I'm just here to listen, I think," he said, sensing how our eyes stuck on him.

"Thanks, Dooley. Glad you're here," people said to him, as the custom went.

"What a bunch of horseshit," Nadine said.

"Hi," Wendy said. "Would you like to introduce yourself?"

"I'm new here, too, you know."

A few others tried to say "Welcome" and "Glad you're here" to Nadine, but it came out flat and expectant.

"Typically, at this meeting, we introduce ourselves and share our experience as it relates to alcohol," Wendy said.

"Well, I'm Nadine, okay. I'm from New York, and—"

"Hi, Nadine," we said in unison.

"—think you're a pack of simple fools if you believe thing one out of his mouth. Thing one. Seriously."

"Aw shit, Nadine. This ain't about you," Dooley said, smiling. "Unlike every other damn thing."

"No, no. I'm not gonna let him."

"Here we go. Here it comes."

Nothing much like this had ever happened at meetings, as far as I'd seen. Usually we were so wary around our anger that we talked ourselves out of feeling it in the same breath we started with. Directly attacking others was forbidden. Each person's turn was a little lake of sovereign time in which they could cuss the bitch bank teller or gloss on about how their higher power helps with everything, even choosing which sandwich for lunch and so on. It was protocol to let somebody fight through their own talk, no matter how chilling or stupid. Or gilded. You had to find the end of what you were saying by yourself.

"Guys," Wendy said, "you'll have to talk about this outside the meeting."

"Like hell! I got an order to keep him away from me for a reason. For one, my case worker says he can't come in the house unless there's a signed paper."

"Hoo, hoo, hoo," Dooley said. "I'm crying already."

"Let me tell you. I had my babies waiting for him to come back with some milk and things. This was before. So I got to go dig him up from whatever pile of shit he's been sunning himself in, because he forgot. Of course, he's at the bar with his whole paycheck cashed out."

"Least I got a paycheck." Dooley folded his arms up on his gut.

"And I know for a fact," Nadine said, "that he touches little girls. Yes uh-huh he does. I seen him do it too."

Wendy put her hand on Dooley's shoulder and said, "Come on. Jim will go outside with you for a minute." But he smacked her hand away.

"Would you just shut up?" he said to Wendy.

"It's my *turn*, Darrell. It's my fucking turn."

This was so true that it seemed to wear Nadine out. Everybody looked hard into their coffee cups. A few people shrugged at me like I was supposed to handle Nadine since I brought her, but I shrugged back. I didn't know anything about Nadine except she didn't like the Bible and she had called Alan Jackson a big dumb cunt when his song came on the car radio earlier. I had no idea what she was talking about.

Nadine stood up and felt around for her coat. I put it on her shoulders and helped her find my elbow again. Once it was clear that she was done talking, the room said, "Thanks, Nadine" and "Glad to hear you" and "Keep coming back" and all that other shit. We still had to get to the door, though. It was the longest parade I'd ever been in. They couldn't wait for us to go. Nobody could breathe until we were gone.

A little snow started once we were moving again. It tranced through the headlights. I thought of arcade games and crude animation.

We drove on past the highway and I could see the green searchlight on the prison. Off far it looked like it was blinking, but up close in the sweep of the snow you could see that it rotated. On the radio, the call-in show host was saying his mom left him all alone in the hot car while she ran in for groceries all the time and it wasn't a crime back then and didn't he turn out okay all the same.

It was protocol to let somebody fight through their own talk, no matter how chilling or stupid.

"You ever have a piña *colada?*" Nadine asked.

"I was more of a—"

"You ever have a *hurricane?*"

"Just bourbon," I said. "Vodka."

"Vodka," she said. If she said it any harder, she would summon it. God, I was tired of her.

A gray blur skittered across the headlights and I twitched the steering wheel too slow to miss it. I waited for the thump, but there was none.

"Christ," Nadine said.

"Thought I saw a possum."

"I need a bathroom," she said.

"It's only a few miles now."

"Unless you want me to mess your car, I need a bathroom now."

I pulled into the donut shop by the airport and began again to unfold and unbuckle her. The cook inside had his white paper cap and his cigarette. Watching us, he looked like something from an old movie, but he also looked like he knew it. He couldn't possibly need cigarettes to breathe, like I did. He watched me strain to hold the door open with one arm while Nadine tapped her way into the room.

"Just put me in the regular stall," Nadine said. "You don't need to watch me or whatever."

The bathroom was a big square with only one toilet in it. I described it to her and said I'd be waiting outside. But I didn't leave. I closed the door and stood there without breathing.

Nadine pulled her pants down and right away a big shitting sound ripped out of her.

"Oh boy," she said. How could I not laugh? What was I even doing, standing there? Oh boy is right. Oh boy.

> ## I was a flying five-breasted woman. Believe nothing else. Oh boy!

Sometimes to entertain myself I pretended I was myself of a year ago looking at my present life. Friday night. You would not have been able to convince me this was it. Where were the floods of the city and the neons and the lovely vernacular howling of my people? That's where I belonged. There was a glow in the bottom of a glass, impossibly dark and light at the same time, which lit me and made me blonder and my waist itty-bitty and my hips a brave monument. I was a flying five-breasted woman. Believe nothing else. Oh boy!

The bathroom smelled like clay and clogged drains. I was choking on my spit from holding in laughter.

There were no neons, of course. The only place I ever drank was the Rock Lick, except when I made an excuse to go home and drink alone on the couch. I listened to the same shitty country songs again and again on my laptop. I would wake up and find it crashed sideways on the floor with the gasping autoplay ad for a porn game chiming, starting, ending. The other thing I always watched were demos of very expensive juicers.

"Okay," Nadine yelled, unaware that I was watching her. "I need some help now!"

She had leaned her cane against the wall but it had fallen, I realized, and she stood there on her white prickle-skin legs waiting for me to assist. Her sweatshirt hung down over her crotch. There were some red drops on the toilet seat. She was bleeding through her sweatpants, just a little but I could tell what it was. I was surprised. I'd thought she was older.

"Nadine, uh, do you have a tampon or something in your purse?"

"What!"

"It looks like you're bleeding." I began to fear that I would have to insert it for her. What would I do? My hands were so cold. I didn't want to touch her there. I could run hot water over my fingers in the sink to warm them. But then I realized how unnecessary that would be. She still had her hands. Maybe I would have to unwrap it for her, though.

"You're sick," she said, and pulled up her sweatpants.

I grew up in a valley, and everything that happened to me there happened so slow it didn't even seem to take place until later. I stomped on hornets. I named countless generations of barn cats, though they were always dying of snakebites and cars and worms and their spines grew bulging and their eyes crumbed over. I made bowls of blue water with food coloring: swimming pools. When the mayapples came up in early summer like a floating green carpet, I lay in them and tried to make myself small. They looked like beach umbrellas from underneath. I drew creatures that were half cat, half mermaid, with clouds of blond pageant hair and crowns and furry little bellybuttons. I ate, alone, whole boxes of rocky road cocoa cookies, which I first rolled into balls so the oil beaded up on the outside. I liked calligraphy and secret codes. I wanted to be an astronomer. I pulled the fat of my stomach away from my body until the skin split in shiny pink seams. Extinction frightened me. I once told my mother I'd volunteer to die on behalf of the human race if it meant the gorillas could stay.

It scared me how these things came back without reason or purpose. It didn't matter what I was doing, who I was talking to.

I watched my mother get ready to go out. She combed her hair over one shoulder and drew her eyebrows in with a little brush. She put a drop of Shalimar down the front of her shirt and on the back of each knee. "So they can smell you when you're walking away," she explained. I helped her match her earrings from a pile of them dumped out on the bedspread and choose between hoops or moons.

Sometimes, when I lit a cigarette while I was driving, I would get caught staring into the flame as it flagged under my nose and find it very difficult to look back up at the road.

Dedlyn Glen and Apartments still glowed in its floodlights, but the kitchen and dining room were dark. I wondered if I should leave Nadine in the same place where I found her. I wanted to prop her up by the door with a note and peel out shrieking onto the highway. Down the hall, a nurse blew her nose in long, thorough rips. She was dispensing dollops of lotion into paper pill cups on a tray and taking notes with a pencil she licked the tip of before writing.

"Excuse me, excuse me!" I yelled down to her.

"Yeah?"

"I brought Nadine back. From the AA meeting."

"Yeah, okay."

"But what do I do with her?"

"Do with her! Don't matter to me."

"I mean, where does she go?"

"Well, anyplace she wants. She can walk, right?"

Nadine dropped her hand from my elbow and went down the dark hallway and into the heart of the home. The tip of the cane skated ahead of her. I hated her again.

"Well, bye," I said.

"Give up," the nurse said.

I went home and fucked Baird. We took off only the necessary clothes, although I pulled up his T-shirt to see the mushroom white of his stomach. It didn't take very long. When we finished, he went back to making pancakes. It was an ongoing experiment. Choco-fruity combo was the best so far.

I liked to stand in the doorway and watch him work. What would I think of him if I didn't know this man? If I saw him from afar? I liked the dark nap of hair on his forearms. I liked the way his hair sat up on his head. He looked a little confused. He gave me a plate of silver dollars.

"So. Babe. I'm going out in a minute. You wanna come?"

"I don't know."

"Glenda said she would make you something. A Shirley Temple or whatever."

"Oh boy."

"Everybody misses you." He landed play punches on my ribs. "A few games of pool and then we come right home."

"Did you ever meet Dooley's wife?"

"Nah. She lives in California, remember?"

"I don't think so."

"Poor guy. He needs to let up a little. I been worried about him a little."

I put my head against his chest and held him. "Let's get a dog," I said.

"Sure. You find us the money, though, first."

"If we don't get a dog, I'm going to shoot my face off."

"Honey, you gotta stop saying things like that." I was going to cry, so I went to do the dishes instead.

"But dogs are free from the pound," I said, "aren't they?"

"A dog's gotta eat," he said. Oh, when men said things like this.

Baird put on his boots and quick grabbed the pint of Ten High like I might not see him doing it. He pulled up the curtain of my hair and kissed the back of my neck.

"You go to those meetings and you come home so sad," he said. "But what you really gotta remember is you're not the same as them, okay? You're just fine."

"Tell them hi for me."

"Always," he said, and left me there.

I turned on some lights but the house was still empty all over. I couldn't sleep sometimes, but I tried anyway to stare at the dark until it convinced me. It would convince me eventually. It was bigger than I was, and cunning. I waited for the moon to fall out of the sky, go blind, go rolling away elsewhere.

the bus

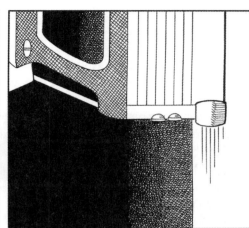
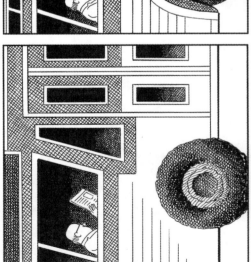

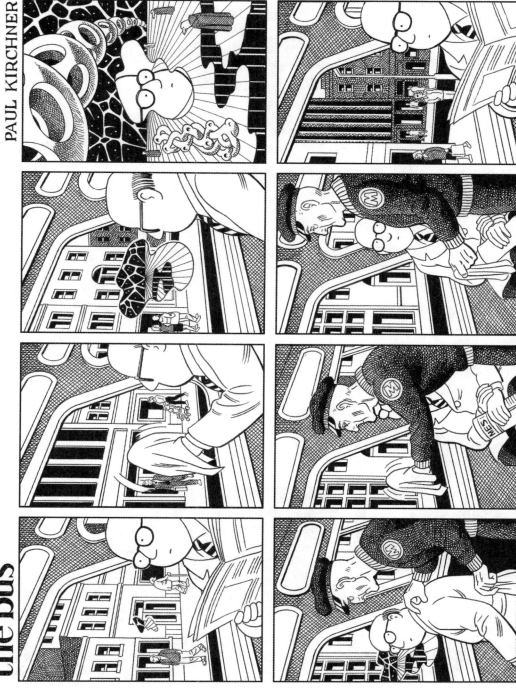

ROOM

Mary Barnett

Here is a place of disaffection

I.

The psychologist's small, perfectly square office reminds me of the dorm rooms back at the Plex, at Connecticut College, where I go to school. The Plex: the dorm nobody wants because the windows don't open and nothing sticks to the walls.

So they've put me in this group.

I've just been evaluated by the staff psychologist and now we've come up front to meet the others.

She swings open a heavy door on our right letting me pass ahead of me into a large stale-smelling room.

"I think you'll add a unique perspective to our group," she says, flattening herself up against the wall like a folded umbrella.

I look back at this pleasant, unremarkable woman I've just met and she snaps into focus. I recognize her shampoo. This is someone I know how to talk to.

"Aren't you coming?" I ask.

"Oh no," she says. "This is what we call a *peer* group."

The women are drinking red cans of Coke, no diet, and chain-smoking cigarettes. I'm judgmental about the Coke. One woman sits sunk in the faux-leather couch, legs tucked up into her sweatshirt, kneecaps punching out the top like breasts. A woman in an oversized parka, hood up, is absentmindedly kicking the underside of the coffee table with her boot, watching a glowing ash disappear deep into the orange pile carpet. Nobody looks up when I come in.

There are six of us. We are the survivors group and I'm looking around and thinking that's a fucking broad category.

This is the Tuesday night Rape or Incest Survivor Group of Greater New London County. The fact that this is the Tuesday night group means that there is also a Thursday night group, and when it turns out that every single one of these women did it or something like it or something worse with their father or their uncle Bob or their brother Seward or Gramps, spread out on some old carpet just like this one, sticky and orange and stained, in the back of the family van, I want a transfer.

We are supposed to be supporting each other. We are supposed to be supporting each other because we have the same issues. We are supposed to be supporting each other because we have the same issues so we can heal.

"I'm Polly," I say and it sounds like a joke. Another year and I will jettison my nursery rhyme nickname. There will be no more putting the kettle on for people. Mary, my proper name, feels restrictive and formal and I like it that way. My rib cage shears forward and I sniff my breath in like a queen. Thirty years later I will learn that renaming oneself is a common reaction to sexual assault. Or perhaps it is part of the cure. It's hard to know.

"I go to Conn. I mean Connecticut College."

I'm about to graduate and want to say I'm going to be an ex-Conn, but I realize no one will think this is funny.

These are not college students.

Susan looks at Danielle. Susan has brown curly hair and is wearing something purple that fits. With jewelry. Everyone else looks unemployed. This makes me think that Susan is the leader and is being paid but I can't tell. Danielle introduces herself and hugs Susan. Danielle is wearing brown corduroys and a big sweater and is blond. Then Susan hugs Taryn. Taryn is wearing blue jeans and a big sweater and is fat. I'm sitting next to Taryn. I don't want her to hug me. I particularly don't want her to hug me because she is fat. I'm smart and I look out the window at just the right moment so she doesn't. Toneesha and Caprice sit by themselves smoking. They're black. I think they are trying to light the carpet on fire.

Susan says she accepts being a survivor with pride. It's who she is. Danielle and Taryn applaud.

"I come here to be with people who understand," Susan says and starts to cry. Maybe she isn't being paid.

We are what my psychology textbook refers to as a "cohort." I do not like my cohort and I do not want my cohort to understand this right away. Caprice and Toneesha obviously think the whole thing is a joke. They know they aren't going to survive.

"Okay, so . . . I was raped," I say next but it sounds like a question. I don't believe it. I'm having a hard time with the word *rape*. It isn't a good word. It doesn't convey the specificity of what occurred.

"I was asleep," I say. "Asleep in my own bed. I live off campus. I have my own apartment. A little house."

They don't seem impressed.

"I was asleep. Someone jumped on top of me. It was Halloween."

I don't say that it was my first apartment. That I had made my own bed frame out of plywood and cinder blocks. That I'd sewn two calico sheets together to make a mattress cover so it could double as a couch in the daytime. That he said, "Give me some pussy."

We are the survivors group and I'm looking around and thinking that's a fucking broad category.

The police took all that down to the police station: my sheets, my flannel nightgown, my yellow stuffed dog, and a document with my signature on it, saying one of my windows wasn't locked. Maybe everything is still down at some police station in a back room in a box with my name on it.

"Did you know him?" Susan asks me and everyone perks up. They're ready to accept me.

"No," I say and breathe in and they breathe out and sit back, bored.

My night of terror feels insignificant in this room. Pulp fiction. Something unpleasant and invasive, but finite, like having your purse snatched. Something only a college student would mind.

"Well," says Susan, "you've come to the right place." She leans forward. Her perfume, something sharp and sweet, releases from an intimate fold.

I look down at my hiking boots. Dark green suede. I wear them to feel game but I haven't been hiking since I was a kid. I'm afraid of twisting an ankle. I'm a senior dance major at Connecticut College, majoring in dance because I want to feel my body and make it say what I want it to say. Finally make it say *yes*.

It's Danielle's turn. She slams the table hard and I jump and she screams *That fucking asshole* and Susan is saying *Let it out* and looping her cigarette in giant circles for emphasis like some guy conducting Barry Manilow on TV.

If I stay here, I'm going to have to start smoking, I think.

Nobody's talking now and the smoke clears and I'm thinking about my mother. She's listed in the Boston Social Register, polite society's list of old families with old money. It's something you are born into.

I called her the next morning. The morning after. The morning after spending all night in the overlit emergency room at the Lawrence and Memorial Hospital being poked, prodded, combed, and flushed. I told her I needed to tell her something but couldn't do it over the phone. She was wary, afraid of being manipulated. She agreed to meet me at Dunkin' Donuts, a place she'd never been; halfway to Providence.

"Mom," I start. And the word sits small and round on my tongue; inert, like a lozenge, from my life before.

"Mom . . . someone broke into my apartment last night."

Some bitterly familiar part of me hopes she'll feel guilty for not driving the whole way.

"I was raped."

And my voice loses its footing there among the donuts.

"Oh, Pols," she says and steps back. She is pressed up against the soda case. Her ten-year-old, overstuffed L. L. Bean parka, good to forty-five degrees below zero, is backlit, framed by tiny plastic bottles of OJ.

"That's the worst thing that can happen to a woman."

"May I help you?" the donut girl says.

My mother looks up, startled to find herself at a counter. She is disoriented for only a moment. Then her smile flashes and her big eyes widen. She loves an audience.

"And what would *you* recommend?" she says brightly, as if ordering a specialty roast from our neighborhood market.

"What a perfectly aw-ful smell," my mother says a few minutes later as I follow her outside. Her Boston Brahmin accent is broad and dramatic. I can't help myself. I love listening to her.

"But that glazed thing was positively scr-rumptious!"

She stops suddenly, sucking in the cold, sweet air. I bump into her.

"Thank *God* it wasn't your sister."

"I don't think I belong here," I say after the requisite bathroom break to Taryn and Susan and Toneesha and now Lauren. She's just come in. She's about my age and has two kids at home. She's getting a restraining order against her husband. She has a sippy cup in her purse.

I am remembering how I went to private school and there were only thirteen kids in my eighth-grade class and if you were in the A group that meant you were smart and you got to read e e cummings and study Bob Dylan as if he were a real poet. Maybe it *wasn't* a person, I'm thinking. Maybe it was a goat. Maybe some rabid goat broke loose from some reject farm down on Route 32.

"We are here to support you," Susan says sympathetically. "We think perhaps you are in denial. We think perhaps something like this happened to you before."

Maybe in the kind of place you're from, I'm thinking, where people have sex with animals when their kids aren't available and that goat fucking had to have me.

Then I remember his hands around my throat. I was screaming and then I

My night of terror feels insignificant in this room. Pulp fiction.

couldn't scream. My muscles let go. Part of my mind slides over to let something else through. Slipping down off the side of the bed. Lower, I think, get lower so there is nothing more to get. My voice smooths itself like a skirt. I plead. Demurely. I have stopped breathing and a minute goes by and I haven't said anything. Susan is still looking at me. I decide I need another approach.

"Okay, maybe I'm angry," I say.

I'll say anything never to see this carpet again. There is smoke rising from between Toneesha's knees.

His arm looked dark against the fluorescent white of his T-shirt, the way everything looks dark when you can't see anything. The way everything looks black when you can't see anything.

Was he black? I don't know but I think so. It was how he spoke. Can I say that? That he sounded black? Some of these women are black. He was inside me but I couldn't feel anything. Sometimes I still can't feel anything.

I went back to the house, only once, before Thanksgiving, with my parents, to pick up my books. As if Proust could help me figure this out. That afternoon, my mother, trying in her own way to be helpful, used her prodigious head, the one that went to Bennington.

"Oh, Pols," she said with feeling, putting *To the Lighthouse* on the top of the pile, "blacks have been subjected to such violence and degradation in our society. Do you think rape could be their way of striking back?" She waited expectantly for my answer as if she were the host of an NPR talk show and I was the expert guest.

"You really should have gone to Bennington," she says over dinner that night at Chuck's Steakhouse in New London, where I've been allowed to order the filet mignon for the first time. "This would never have happened in Vermont."

I'm staring at the clock over Toneesha's head. Waiting for that moment when the minute hand jerks. Susan is still looking at me. Her eyes look all wet. Oh God, she wants to hug me.

Lower, I think, sinking deeper into my chair. Sink lower. So there is nothing more to get. Like that time when my brothers wouldn't stop tickling me and their fingers raced between my legs and I couldn't breathe and finally I slid down onto the floor so they'd lose interest.

"Pipe down!" my mother yelled up the stairs. My parents were watching NOVA and it was a really good one about laterality and brain development.

And my voice smoothed itself like a skirt.

At dinner, my brothers sit smug and silent.

"You egg them on," my mother says. "You know you do. When you scream, you egg them on."

"Say 'uncle,'" my brothers say. "Say 'uncle' and we'll stop!"

Susan is telling me what I need to do in order to heal.

"Say it," my brother says.

Very slowly I am standing. Very slowly, I am standing up and walking toward the door.

"I think I need individual treatment," I say as if I've made an informed decision and a follow-up appointment is already penciled in.

"Uncle, fucking uncle," I think.

Lauren looks up at me then. Her pale nostrils flare. Rhythmically. Reminding me of something. Irregular yellow smoke rings hover at her nostrils and float up into her hair.

It's going to take practice.

But I want to learn how to do that.

II.

On the beach in Virgin Gorda, where my parents take my sister and me on a rape recovery vacation over Christmas, I kiss a Jamaican man named Rocky. He has been pursuing me for days. My parents seem relieved. God forbid I turn into a racist. His lips are unnaturally warm and enveloping, like a woman's vulva, I think. *Vulva* is a new word I've learned to say in therapy.

"Pussy, pussy, pussy," I hiss on the inside.

"Has it occurred to you," Dr. Gottlieb says eventually, 137 sessions in, "that it is indeed the fertile soil this trauma has landed on that has made it persist for so long?"

This is the single longest sentence I've ever heard him speak. And I can't stand the word *fertile* especially spoken by a man with no socks. So I stand up and hit him over the head with my purse. This takes us both by surprise.

The next week he asks me to go back to sitting in a chair.

"I don't think you can handle the couch," he says mildly.

Dr. Gottlieb is tall and quiet and wears no socks and I'm like, what's with the socks, and he sits there and says nothing and I'm angry at him for the first ten sessions and then it's ten years and I'm not all that angry anymore and then I'm dating some guy who calls his penis the "toy cannon" and then I'm not anymore and I cry all the time and then I'm just angry at all the money I've spent in therapy and that I've wasted my youth. That I've wasted my youth just talking about it.

"And then what happened?" he says.

"I called my mother, you know, the one listed in the Boston Social Register."

"Is there another one?" he says.

"No, just that one," I say.

And eventually I don't need to talk about her anymore.

We talked together weekly: Monday 11:00, Tuesday 10:10, Wednesday 3:25, Friday 4:00, for thirty-three years.

We met for twenty years in one room and thirteen years in another room. There was a glitch in my insurance and it paid for most of it. It didn't pay for my pregnancies or childbirth but it paid for therapy. At some point he married a happy woman in a red sundress. We kept talking. I married a sour-faced guy with a sweet heart and we kept talking. He was sixty-nine and I was fifty-seven and we kept talking. I'd met him when I was twenty-three.

He calls on the phone at our appointed time. He calls on the phone because he has been away for a few weeks. He has been away for a few weeks every six months or so but other than that and six weeks every summer and one year when he tried living with his family on a boat, I go there or he calls, so we talk. He is rather thin. He is getting thinner. He is made of paper. I hear beeps in the background. He has no voice left, just a sort of guttural-sounding croak from being intubated for so long and I keep talking. I tell him about my kids and being annoyed at my husband and how I've been controlling my anger better and am struggling with a paper and I continue to try to find ways to tell him that I have loved him, that I love him, that I will continue to love him, even though I don't use those words in that way. We have this very prescribed relationship. It lasts for fifty minutes four times a week and now it's thirty-four years and his dying means I don't have to stay in that room anymore. I don't have to stay. Thank God I don't have to. Thank God. And I don't want to just talk about me. I'd like to have a conversation for Pete's sake. And then it was Tuesday and he called and I just talked about me.

This is the single longest sentence I've ever heard him speak. And I can't stand the word *fertile* especially spoken by a man with no socks.

There wasn't any other language to speak. It was all I had. I tried to make it mean other things. "Hi. How are you? You sound horrible. I can't understand a word you are saying. What is the matter with you? Is this cancer? I know it's cancer. I know the look and . . ."

"That's not a very nice thing to say," he said once. But then he stopped saying that.

Those were the rules. He said there weren't any rules; that I projected them and held on to them because I wanted control; yet every week we talked in the same room for twenty years and then another room for thirteen years or maybe it was nineteen years at the first house with the room at the top of the stairs and the weird defunct brown stove in the waiting room and the forty-seven *New Yorker* magazines and fourteen years in the long room by the sea with the white carpet and the same old chairs and a painting I didn't much like of some city in the rain. Sometimes he would stand up and pick up a piece of lint from the carpet and then sit back down and he started to wear these knit gloves because his hands had become so thin and so cold. And I talked and I talked and I talked. I knew it was bad the time he didn't stand up when it was time for me to leave because he was so very courtly. When my eyes met his on the way out—or maybe they didn't, maybe I just wished they had—I sort of bowed. After a while it didn't matter what I said so much as that we kept at it.

I'd get all worked up every few years and say, What is this, why are we still doing this, nobody does this anymore, and he would say, We are just talking, and I believed him.

The last time we talked was a week before he died and I was desperate. I couldn't thank him enough because when I thanked him he would just keep listening to me. I wrote something down to stop the flow. "Your listening has allowed me to believe I live inside a bigger listening," I said between beeps.

His wife called four days later and I went to the funeral. I sat at a table with his swimming buddies from high school.

In the final analysis I am left with his intention. He believed in what we were doing together. It absolutely mattered and it was able to matter one hundred percent because it was prescribed and because it was prescribed it was limitless. We never talked about that.

It occurs to me that that room with the uncomfortable furniture was just a waiting room. He waited with me and then it turned out I was waiting with him. A month or so before he died, he pushed himself out of the brown leather chair with the duct tape wrapped around its arms. He looked out of the low window that looked out on Long Island Sound, where, he said, there were seals feeding, but which I could never see. "We are so lucky," he said. 🪦

Cody Carvel

PALACE OF 6TH-GRADERS

You can still hear the emergency sirens
When the wind dies down, the only character—
His sticky breathing upon me and his too
Short shorts

I took to wearing over-the-shoes
Roller skates, in the hopes I might be sent over
The edge of the world or

My ark pages long, handwritten and full of intimate
Prophecies:

The blouse of a ghost in the utmost invisible
Ghost town. But no, nothing from nothing
Was born here today.

Or the whoosh of the fan, a choir:
"You were born to be a victim, baby,
Or nothing at all . . ."

They wink as though we are in
On the same secret, to suggest
They know mine.

TULIP MANIA

Oh Mary we will probably not live
To see the next century's nineties.
Our century's nineties were grand.
They were ok. They were before
The End Times and Now
I'm in a fit about not ever getting to find out if our nineties were better

And now now
I have this crown imperial to put in your hair and then to put in my hair and
then to trade several times so
We can both see how being with a beautiful thing looks
Impromptu magic

Like the magician I was seeing before
Slavery got all popular again. He would find a currency
From the vicinity of my ear and I
Would tell him to let it collect a little
Interest. Beautiful rascal, beautiful
Marquis, beautiful got your nose, beautiful time and hat and we were
In the company collecting a garnishment, in the company now
Tulips are again collecting interest.

I know we will live among tulips, though
The Southern solstice is giving
Me fits. And if the tulips go
On forever-hiatus I will sing us into primers—
(The Discovery, Cultivation, and Subsequent Invention by Mary and Peg) Of Tulips, True and Miraculous,
Which begins:

Of Tulips

A dream I have most nights
We're angels
No more like
Carrier pigeons

At best
   Bats

But
For once
From now on we're goin
Enrobed englobed bedeckt

And fly fly fly

FICTION

Treasure
State

Smith Henderson

John went to visit his father in the prison hospital. The old man sat up against a pile of gray pillows. There were dark half-moons under his eyes, and the skin around his mouth was purple and yellow like he'd been hit there. He breathed heavily through cracked and bloody lips.

"Lookit you," the old man said. "You're all growed and swole up." He looked at John's arms.

"You can't come live with us," John said.

His father fixed him with an expressionless gaze that conveyed nothing but the monstrous obstinacy that had landed him in prison in the first place. It was supposed to be for life.

"You tell your mother?" he said.

"She knows I'm here."

The son of a bitch pushed himself up, and it took something out of him to do so. He panted slowly for a moment.

"She agreed to it already, don't you know," his father croaked.

John looked off, away from his emaciated father, the bruised face, the cracked lips, and the hairline crossing the high crown of the older man's head. What all cancer had done to his once handsome features.

"You better get used to it," his father said, his lips drawing back in a dry grin. "I'm awn die in that house a mine."

John and his brother, Daniel, left the next day. They pulled out of their little place in Gnaw Bone, Indiana, and drove through the hills they'd coursed as boys, farther, to woods they knew less well, and then they were on a plain country road through abject farmland, foreign odors blowing through the windows. John said they were better off traveling the back roads.

Outside of Adolf, Indiana, they stopped for lunch in a diner choked with senior citizens.

"What can I get?" Daniel asked. He was fifteen and had been suspended from school for fighting.

"Anything."

"Anything?"

"Yeah."

"But you said we don't got more'n eighty dollars to make it the whole way."

"I said we weren't making it the whole way on eighty dollars. You got to listen."

Daniel looked at the menu and then at his brother, who was reading through the local paper, the *Adolf Announcement*. He asked John what he was reading for. Daniel wouldn't even open a book unless it looked like it might have pictures in it.

"Just order," John said, nodding toward the waitress who was standing there. She was pretty, given the town. She had close-set eyes and a wreckage of teeth, but still looked okay to a kid from Gnaw Bone. Daniel ordered a Denver omelet with no peppers or onions, a side of bacon, and a chocolate shake. John said he'd have black coffee and pancakes.

> Daniel wouldn't even open a book unless it looked like it might have pictures in it.

"She's awful cute," Daniel offered, as she went to get John's coffee. "Can we take her with us?" He wiggled his eyebrows like an idiot.

"Why'd you order a Denver omelet if you were just going to have them make a ham and cheese?"

"We're going to Denver, ain't we?"

"No."

"Well, it's in Montana, ain't it?"

"No. It *ain't*. Jesus. How dumb are you?"

"Pretty goddamn dumb," Daniel said.

"Well, see if you can at least wrap your mind around this," John said, pointing at an obituary. "Says here the service is in about an hour."

People being the way they are, few realized that their dead had been robbed. They returned from the funeral and set out the cold cuts on the silver trays, the faceted glasses, and the punch. They stocked bottles of beer and cans of Coke in buckets of ice, smoked a quick cigarette out back, and met the grief-stricken, the condolers, and the well-wishers at the door. The furniture smelled of the person they'd just praised to heaven and commended to the dirt. The mourners assembled along the walls in grim or conversant clusters depending on their affinity with the dead and the yet living. Then they stole away to the upstairs bedroom or the chest in the basement or the desk in the study, only to discover the particular heirloom missing. And the surprise turned hot, and they tiptoed out of the room, slowly pinched closed the door, went up or down the stairs, and took their spot along the wall. They glowered at their kin, wondering which one had got there first.

A few days later, John and Daniel were pressing on to Long Creek to fence the things in the backseat. A fur coat, a sword, three crystal glass cats, and a variety of other finds that might have been worth something or nothing at all, it was hard to tell.

Daniel paused at her door, and winked at his brother, but John pulled him along.

John asked how much they had and Daniel opened the glove box and pulled out the transparent bank-tube canister. They put money in it now, but when they'd found the canister in a bottom drawer back in Weston, it was full of empty prescription bottles. There was a lot of weird shit in bottom drawers. Daniel twisted open the canister and counted the bills.

"Not great. About a hundred-twenty-something."

"Let's just see what we get for this stuff in Long Creek," John said.

"I dunno," Daniel said.

"Don't know what?"

"We're doing this, then? We're not going back?"

"You wanna live with that piece of shit?"

"I ain't afraid of him."

"Lookit you, big man. You wanna go back and kill him, then?"

Daniel sighed at the endless farmland ahead of them.

"There's no speed limit in Montana, you know," said John.

"You already said."

"Marijuana is legal there." John adjusted the rearview mirror. "We have to, we can sleep in the car."

"But you said we shouldn't sleep on the road. That was a rule, you said."

"Let's just see what we get for this stuff in Long Creek."

They chose Montana because of the way the word sounded and because they'd been to Chicago and had formed opinions about cities. A city was a terrible thing, but Montana sounded romantic and open, the opposite of Gnaw Bone, which sounded like something a dog was doing.

In a town called Oscarville they took too long. Or else the funeral was shorter than normal. A car door closed. Footsteps on the porch, voices downstairs. They waited until it was quiet, then slunk to a rear window. But after they jumped off the sloping roof of the back porch and landed in the yard, a woman came out the back door and started at the sight of them standing there. Then she collected herself and said everyone was gathering in the living room. She held open the door for them, and they were obliged to go into the house they had been burgling just moments before.

"And how did you know Gary?" the woman asked, almost greedily, as might one who had just lost a loved one and wanted to savor every last instance of the dead person's intimacies, however slight.

John looked at Daniel and then coughed into his hand.

"From the youth center, I'll bet," she said.

"Yes, ma'am," John said. "The youth center."

Daniel grinned helpfully.

"That man," she said, squeezing their forearms.

They went down a narrow hall, past a rolltop desk that had nothing of value in it, and a bedroom where a teenaged girl now sat on a bed. Daniel paused at her door, and winked at his brother, but John pulled him along.

In the living room congregated about fifteen people of approximately the same age as the woman—John guessed seventy—some of whom rose slowly from their chairs, asked John and Daniel their names, shook their hands, and said nice things about the youth center over in Benton County, wherever that was. John and Daniel said they weren't hungry, but someone brought John a plate of cake and baby carrots anyway. Daniel said again that he didn't want anything to eat, and for a moment they were alone along the wall.

"I'monna hit the head, John."

"Just hold it. We're getting out of here in a minute."

"I gotta go," Daniel said, slipping John's reach.

Daniel stopped at the room where the girl was still sitting on the bed and leaned against the jamb. She didn't notice him right away. She wore a plain black dress, but her hair had green streaks in it. Her cowboy boots were shiny as wet tar. Eyes within dark makeup flashed when she noticed him there. He was neither especially handsome nor dynamic, but now had an aura of freedom and outlawry about him.

"Hey," he said.

She sat up straight. He could see her black bra strap where it separated from the strap of her dress.

"I'm Dan."

"Hi Dan."

"Hi."

"I'm Gwen."

"Well, hi Gwen."

They smiled at each other.

"You wanna go outside?" he asked.

"Only if I never come back in," she said.

She reached under her bed and drug out an olive duffel that had things written all over it in black marker.

"Do you have a car?" she asked.

"Uh-huh."

"Take me somewhere."

Daniel turned around to get a view of the front room and his brother, but he couldn't see through the throng. It appeared that a lot of kids from the outlying towns who'd gone to the youth center had arrived. The bedroom window was open and she'd thrown her bag through it.

"Hold up," Daniel said, and climbed out after her.

She was originally from Baltimore but the Treasure State sounded just fine to her. She said no funny business, she didn't put out, and that she'd give him money for the ride. She seemed almost expert at negotiations of this sort. Daniel could not believe this was in fact happening. The overwhelming actuality of a girl. He let her in the backseat of the car, put her bag in next to her, and jumped in the passenger seat.

"What's all this stuff?"

"Our things."

"A menorah?"

"A what?"

She held up the brass menorah. He shrugged.

"Why are you in the passenger seat?" she asked.

"My brother'll be here in a minute."

He yearned toward the front door for his brother to come out.

"How'd you know my uncle?"

"I didn't."

"What do you mean you didn't?"

"Just never mind. Here comes John."

Daniel could see John mouthing *Hell no*.

He got in. "Hell no," he said. "Sorry hon, but no."

"Why not?" Daniel asked.

"Are you stupid?" He turned all the way around in the seat. "You need to exit this vehicle. Now."

"Come on, John. We already busted into the pl—"

"Dan! Jesus. Shut up."

Her eyes pinged between the two of them.

"Were you two robbing our house?"

John took off his sunglasses and squeezed the bridge of his nose. Then he got out, opened the back door, yanked her bag into the street, and reached in for her. She slid to the other side and kicked at him.

She said no funny business, she didn't put out, and that she'd give him money for the ride.

"I'll tell!" she said. John stopped trying to get her. He stood and looked out over the car to the house, where the people were gathered inside, and then up the block, where no one was ever about in any of these towns. Everyone was at a funeral or a wake. He knew immediately why the girl was running away. He ducked back down.

"You'll do what you'll do. But you're coming out of there one way or the other."

"You're a fuckin' dick, man," she said.

"You'll see I'm worse than that. You got two seconds before I pull you out by that green hair. I shit you not, girl."

She glared at him, and when he grabbed at her, she knocked his hand away and let herself out the passenger side. John got in, started the car, and pulled out. Daniel watched her gather her bag and the things that had spilled from it into the road.

There was a night when John had a hammer in his bed and promised himself that he would kill the old man if he came into their room again. He was about twelve years old and there wasn't anything he wanted more than his father's death.

It was Daniel who always got the brunt of it. Something about Daniel's softness and curiosity just enraged the old man. Even things that weren't his fault. Things John had done. Left a toy in the yard or forgot to turn off the sprinkler. Their father would go after Daniel even if John tried to take the blame.

Times, he wished his father would come after him instead. It was so much worse to be afraid for Daniel than for himself.

So he'd taken the hammer from the shed. Practiced hitting the pumpkins in Cartwright's field, the peen chopping into the shell, ripping out the stringy orange meat and seeds. Tore up a half acre.

The next day his mother cleaned up while they were at school. Sheets changed, toys put away. When they got home, the hammer was gone, not in the shed, nowhere.

The skin on the back of John's head tingled at the sight of her.

In Juniper they sold a Polaroid camera and several box sets of VCR tapes. It was wet but not presently raining and they perched on a wet stone bench in front of the courthouse. A cop came out of the building, descended the marble steps, and nodded at them. When he was out of sight, they went to their car and left town.

They found a KOA and set up a moldering tent they'd stolen from a garage in a small town called Wellington. They cooked pilfered hot dogs over a campfire and ate them rolled in slices of white bread they'd also stolen and drank water from the nearby spigot. They didn't even have a cup.

"I thought we'd be in Montana by now," Daniel said.

"We need to get a little more money to make a run at it."

"Can't we just do this all the way out there?"

"The towns get farther apart out west."

"Oh."

The fire snapped out a small red coal near John's foot.

"We're still going to Littleton tomorrow."

"Yup."

John put out the coal with his heel.

"I wonder if that girl is okay," Daniel said.

"You're wondering if her tits are okay."

"She didn't turn us in."

"You don't know that."

"We'd of been arrested by now."

John studied the fire. Daniel stood.

"Not everybody is a son of a bitch, John."

"I'm just trying to protect you."

"I'd like to know what the hell from."

Daniel stomped off to the tent, and John sat by the fire, feeding it for a few hours until he ran out of sticks. He went in to sleep, but only turned on the ground and listened to Daniel's untroubled breathing. It was pure luck that the old man had been caught red-handed and went down. Though it galled John that a broken taillight saved them. And even though John had seen with his own eyes that their father was in no condition to come after them, nor really had a reason to, the fear of the man kept him awake just the same.

He went out in the brush for more firewood and brooded over the fire until morning.

John found a pawnshop in Littleton to sell a sword, the *American History of Folk Music*, and several rings. The man slowly counted out five twenties, and over his glasses watched John, who was pacing off his nerves. John could see small alarms going off in the pawnbroker's eyes, could sense it coming.

"These things are yours to sell, right?"

John strode over to the counter.

"You want them or not?"

"Well, now I'm sure I don't know."

John swept the rings into his hand and stuffed them into his jeans, tucked the LPs under his arm, and gathered up the sword and scabbard, all the while glaring at the clerk, expecting the man to stop him. But he didn't.

"Asshole," John said.

"Get on out of here before I call the cops."

The sun quaked overhead and the light flashing off the worn white roadway was too much to even look around. He made straight for the car. He tossed the sword and the records into the trunk and slid into the front seat, but Daniel was not inside and nowhere about. He pulled his sunglasses from behind the visor and went to look for his goddamn brother.

He walked up the block past the pawnshop onto a main street that was nearly abandoned save a few cars parked on the main drag, one of which was a squad car with a policeman in it. He nodded at the policeman and crossed the street and felt the cop's eyes on him the whole way as he passed the closed-up storefronts and peered uselessly into the tinted opaque windows of the bars for his brother. This was pointless. He stopped in the middle of the sidewalk and immediately started walking back to the car, patting his pockets and pantomiming that he'd forgotten his wallet.

The girl, Gwen, was sitting on the hood of the car, her legs crossed behind Daniel, who stood between them. The skin on the back of John's head tingled at the sight of her. Daniel turned around.

"Now look, John. You might as well know right now that she comes with us or I want half my money and we'll go our separate ways."

John ignored him and went around and got in the driver's seat. Daniel opened the passenger door. The squad car slid past, the cop looking in their direction, and Daniel's voice was lost in John's ears. This was real trouble, you could see how it would go down, right here in Littleton: the runaway with seaweed streaks in her hair, the suspicious pawnbroker, the squad car slowing to stop, red-and-blues lit up. Just like the old man.

"Get in," John said.

"I mean it, John. I'm not gonna let you leave her here—"

"Just get in!"

Daniel and Gwen hopped in the back together with her bag. John pulled out of the lot and went up the street. Nothing happened. He took to the highway and nothing happened. They drove for two hours, nothing happened. They weren't pulled over, they weren't surrounded as he filled the tank in Ballinger, and they weren't dragged from the tent in the night. Their father didn't materialize out of the dark, fumy and distorted with rage. But John did not sleep, such was his dread.

John could hear them kiss with glacial quiet so as not to wake him, and when they could take it no longer, they snuck out to the car to do it. But the rear window was cracked open and he could hear their moans as the car gently rocked like a boat in a wake, and when they were finished, John could hear her quietly crying and Daniel saying things in a slow, sad way, how a person might talk to a wounded animal or a child who was stuck in a well. Somehow Daniel was good, a good person. And John felt terrifically alone and strained to hear exactly what they communed, but it wasn't for him however much he might want, deserve, or need it, people don't get what they deserve, everything oh every last thing is given out at random.

They were nearing a town called Casper that John said might be promising when Daniel asked why they weren't going west. Gwen had taken the map and was having Daniel pose her questions.

"We are going west."

"I don't think so," Daniel said, looking at the place she pointed to on the map.

"Casper is east of us," Gwen said. "It's not even a day away from Indiana."

John turned on the radio, panned the dial for something to listen to.

"We're going in circles," Gwen said.

The house in Casper was locked, but John got on a milk crate and pried open the bathroom window with a crowbar. He squirmed through the hole and peeked back out at his brother below. He told him to go wait in the car.

"What? Fuck that."

"Honk twice if you see anything."

John closed the window on his brother's protests and strode briskly down the hall. At the end were two bedrooms. One was a child's room. A small table. Bunk beds. Vases, flowers, scrapbooks. There were balls of tissue and pictures of the children were fanned out over the floor next to a half glass of wine.

> He wondered how she couldn't sense him under there, hear him breathing, feel his body heat.

John didn't understand until he went into the other room. On the bed were two black dresses, and shoes spilled out of the closet. When he realized what had happened to the children he couldn't seem to get enough air and the inside of his chest felt like a twisted bedsheet. He sat on the floor, his vision pinholed, taking big lungfuls of air.

When he felt okay again, he stood. His head was a heavy gourd and he was very tired. He looked inside the closet and the dresser and saw no clothes for a man. He sat on the bed and dropped back onto the dresses and bedclothes. The air was cool and still and no sound punctured the air's dull nothing hum. His heartbeat slowed. He was very tired.

There had been two sharp honks but he only remembered the sound of them when he heard the front door opening. The pad of feet on the runner in the hall. He rolled off the bed and scuttled under it just as a woman came in, pulling off her pumps. She unzipped, and her dress fell smartly to the floor. She left the room, and he started to slide out from under the bed, but she immediately returned and he wriggled back underneath. She sat down and opened a drawer in the bedside table. She got all the way on the bed and was at something, but he could not tell what. In a few moments, he heard a lighter and smelled marijuana. She moved against the headboard and smoked. There was a knock at the front door, but she was still and he was still. He wondered how she couldn't sense him under there, hear him breathing, feel his body heat. He could tell everything she was doing and she had no idea he was down there. Another knock. He wondered if it was Daniel. *Go away*, he thought, even though he wanted to escape. *Leave her alone.*

She lit the joint again and smoked and for long minutes it was quiet. He couldn't think of a way to reveal himself that wouldn't scare the hell out of her. He would've liked to explain. Apologize, even commiserate. But it would be unbearably cruel to scare her now.

A long, thin sound as through reed without an instrument escaped her and turned into a slow moan and then outright sobbing. Heaving. The covers churned up as she must have been clutching and writhing in them. By the way the bed sometimes bounced under her, the mattress sagging and just kissing his chest when she did so, he imagined her pelvis high up and then dropping.

For minutes she was still, and then she would remember or want to cry some more and she would start up again. Hours it went like this. The house would go still for so long that he thought she might be asleep, and he would be about to slide out from under the bed, and she would begin sobbing again. So often that he quit feeling bad for her. So often that it was now dusk, now dark, now the bottomless night.

He woke to her breathing, slow and steady, the sleeper's breathing. He moved out from under the bed, crouched where he could see the back of her head. He wanted to pet her brown hair, to see her face. He bear-crawled to the door. In the hall he stood. A truck somewhere outside shifted gears and he waited until it passed, then unlocked the front door, closed it softly behind him, and strode out into the naked day.

He went up the street, refreshed from the sleep that'd been forced on him, the first good sleep in a long time. He felt okay.

He spotted the car in front of a café. They wanted to know where he'd been, what had happened to him. He looked like shit, they said. He told them to order him a coffee and went to the bathroom to wash his face.

He drove all day and through the night, his brother and Gwen curled up in the backseat asleep. He pulled into town, got a local paper, and scanned the obituaries. The day was dawning. He took the county road and stopped by the field.

Daniel woke up, got out to pee, and then sat on the rear bumper with his brother.

"What the fuck are we doing?" Daniel asked.

"You remember when I busted up all those pumpkins?"

"With the hammer?"

"The old man beat the hell out of you for it. Even though I did it."

The patch had already been harvested, Cartwright's pickup in the field, the trailer full of pumpkins. Daniel's sigh steamed out into the cold air.

"So you're going over there," he said.

John nodded.

"You don't need to."

"You two can just drop me off."

"We can just keep going."

John looked over at his brother. "He has it coming, Dan."

John went inside, where his father lay on the couch in the throes of his last fever. The sound of the screen door clapping shut and the sight of his son startled him.

"What in the hell are you at?" he rasped. "Sneaking in here like this."

His father reached under the cushions and drew out an old revolver, but it promptly slipped from his hand onto the hardwood floor, thudding harmless as a hammer. The old man didn't reach for it, he was too winded even from this effort. The air rattled in and out of him, his eyes watered from an undisclosed agony. When John stepped forward to pick up the gun, his father's eyes raced about for something to defend himself against this inevitability.

But John noticed how little his father's fear or this profound reversal pleased him and he just stood there, waiting for rage as one might a train on a platform.

"Do what you come to do!" his father hissed.

John went out onto the porch, the old man coughing terribly. He waved at Daniel and Gwen to go on. Daniel scowled and then backed out and drove away, and John realized how he must've looked to them with the pistol, like all kinds of trouble, but the old man was well killed already and there was nothing to be afraid of, nothing to do but see him off. 🛡

FENG SHUI IN THE SPIRIT HOUSE
OF THE NEW FAMILY

Part of the charm of the place in the beginning—wisteria root growing into
   the foundation of the western wall,

old broken furniture piled inside, wild grape high and thick on the hill out
   back.
You couldn't reach through prickly raspberry canes to the grapes,

yellow finches, loud doves, mockingbirds mocking, sparrows, orioles
ate the berries first,
birds before humans in the old order of things,

like the fox with three bumbling kits in the woods of my past life.
A small family in the dappled pattern of spring without
human consciousness,

without malaria pills and global this and that and the first lady's affordable
mustard-colored clothes.

Who was J. Crew? Who was the first decoder of the language
of glaciers, who can make me the horseshoe crab's armor, reverse

the extrusion that turns chicken
into nuggets fingers poppers in the bright diabetic light
of a Colonel?

When the charm wore off I ransacked time,

threw out rugs, beds marked by bats, field rats, squirrels,
the green mildewed couch, nests of fur, seeds, shredded magazines.

My husband listened to love songs, Lucinda Williams'
scratchy, shot-glass keening.

Rain came in through the skylight, at night a reality show of stars and
dark matter.

In my arms I held the mop and broom. I got a wet vac
because there were tears everywhere,

wasps in the stove, webs everywhere, inside my stepdaughter's dollhouse
where once there had been order

and now there was none and the none
became the new order—
overturned chairs, the brothers gone to war, stairs far away from the landing.

Under the wild grape, the heartbreaking beauty of violets,
horseweed in the garden the bees loved.

A young friend came over, *take something*,
we said, and of course she went to the dollhouse to choose.

Would it be a plate from the small dusty table,
or the clock stopped at two on the wall?
Would she take a blanket as big as a stamp for the winters

of the miniature world

or the lamp in the nursery lit by imaginary good night kisses,
the small deck of cards with the queen missing?

No, she took the dice,
she left the mark of her instinct, her vision.
What was tiniest was most important.

We would have to figure out what else was needed.
We would have to start over.

RESPECT THE FACE

Two big men, side by side on the rocking train. One had a tattoo. Both
wore huge versions

of my old boots. The largest had a voice that ratcheted back
        and forth the length of the car. Broad forehead, muscular jaw, like he'd
grown up having to chew whatever life threw

at him, grind it down, make it palatable. The more he talked, the louder his
voice got.
        Sixteen now, he said about his daughter. *My wife gets a little*

carried away with her but not me. I'll swat her butt or kick her legs or even,
        if she needs it, punch her stomach or an arm but not the face.
Respect the face.

I waited for his friend to end it, to speak. His elbows dug into his knees.
His body
        tightened up. Imperceptibly, like he was
ducking something. Not the violence of his friend but something else,

something coming from me.

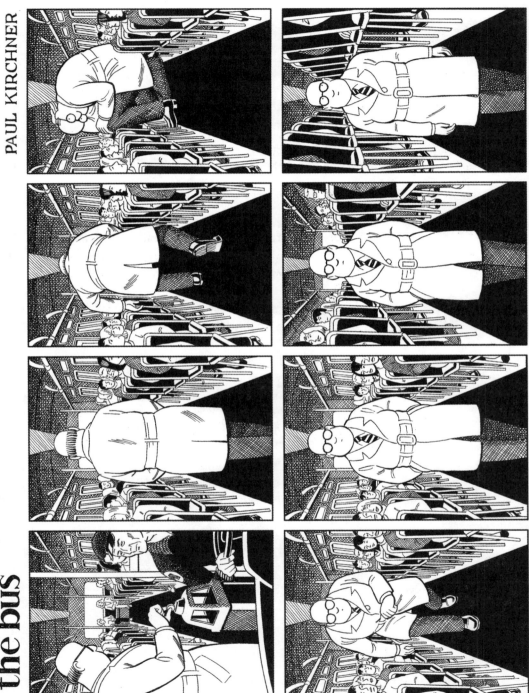

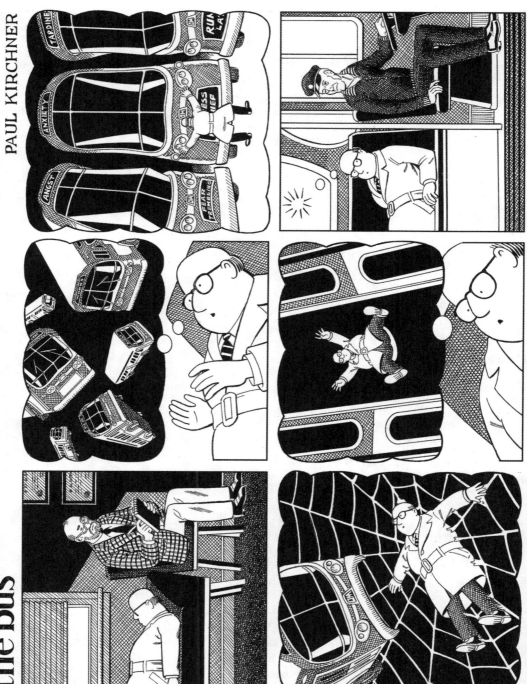

NEW VOICE FICTION

American Tramplings

The tramplings started in Chicago. Five dead, twenty-two injured on May first. The city was adding a station to the red line, north of downtown. Passengers were to get off at Sheridan Station, and if they needed to continue north, there were shuttles ready to take them. This is where the trampling happened. The station's doors were too narrow, the shuttles were right there, waiting. In early June, three dead, forty-seven injured at a Brad Paisley concert in Maryland, at Merriweather Post Pavilion. Sparks from the stage, fire, fear. At a Giants game in August, thirteen dead, thirty injured at AT&T Park in San Francisco after the upper bleachers emitted a volcanic creak and drooped an inch. They were called "tramplings" and they were called by their locations—Sheridan, Merriweather, AT&T. Talk of the tramplings lingered all summer.

Matthew Socia

The tramplings were why Colin phoned me the day after AT&T: to strike hard the public fear and make a new documentary. Colin's habit is to hire a new crew for every film. For his own reasons, though, he rehires me each time. I am his sound guy. I attach microphones to shirts, or sometimes wrap them in lube-free condoms and stick them in the ground. When I need to, I advise him on ambient noise, and I'm always ready to wield a boom pole. After AT&T, we met at an Olive Garden near Stamford. There he talked vaguely of his next project—working title: *Modern Tramplings*—and hired me again. I was happy he'd called. Money had become tight, and Colin's projects pay well. We shop-talked through beers and a basket of breadsticks, and then, before the food came, he gave me money for both of our meals and left. I was not surprised by this, nor did I stew about it as I drove the meals home. This was our relationship. We could move from professional jokeyness to professional surliness without commotion.

Filming started mid-October, a multinational tour: America, America, America, then Europe, Scotland, the Middle East, Russia, island nations, malls, low dark places tapering into small halls, electric bridges, party centers, and, finally, India. Our first location was Cincinnati, but on the plane from LaGuardia Colin talked only about India. He wanted to film India's heat-hovering crowds and people pressed into trains. India, he told me, is the source: where death begins. You think of India, and you think of arms reaching out of colorful fabric, cholera beds, thin men with mustaches dying young. He spoke of leprosy, rabies, tetanus, all flourishing in India. Hundreds of thousands swelling at Hindu gatherings, steep metal stairs at busy stations: tramplings, tramplings. India, he said, will explain to Americans our summer of death.

• • •

We were a small crew. There was Colin, me, the production assistant, the cameraman. Abroad we had a changing guard of translators and facilitators. I avoided the day-to-day bureaucracies of documentary making—earning my check by sneaking away to capture wild sound for the B-roll. I enjoy surprising my directors in postproduction with a hard drive full of all the wild sound they will need. What would a documentary on tramplings be without crowd sounds, car horns, bazaar shouts, and city noisescapes? Colin joined me sometimes after the day's shooting was done, or when he wanted to slip away. In Glasgow, we walked the River Clyde, collecting water and street sounds, and were nearly late for our interview at Ibrox, site of the stadium crush of 1971, sixty-six dead, about two hundred injured.

Ibrox security escorted us to the broad soccer field inside, where we interviewed a woman in her late seventies. Her son had been pinned to a metal staircase and killed. Colin lobbed her questions from behind the camera. He encouraged her to point, gesture, and walk around the field, which presented difficulties for the cameraman. As the sun moved, the stadium's massive shadow unfurled across the grass like a dark sail. The cameraman did his best to shepherd her into sunlight. To help, I blocked her straying path with my boom pole. When the field was fully dark, hours later, we ended the interview. By then the woman was so exhausted by Colin's questioning that she could barely utter her name. We decided to drive her home. She fell asleep in the van, and at her house we asked her husband to rouse her and help her inside.

Later, Colin and I went to a hooligan bar for pub food and beer.

Colin said, "Ibrox. They use the word *crush* for this one. The Ibrox crush. The trampling at Merriweather. It's the Jodhpur stampede, or disaster?"

> **What would a documentary on tramplings be without crowd sounds, car horns, bazaar shouts, and city noisescapes?**

"I think there's differences," I said.

"Ibrox crush. I love how they say *Ibrox* here. They give it like five and a half syllables." Colin squinted an eye and put on a wonderfully fake Scottish brogue. "Ibrox Ibrox Ibrox. Saying it's like eating a pie."

Colin is a stocky guy of princely bearing, almost fifty. He wears a Yankees hat, though I know he couldn't name anyone on the team. "Ibrox," he said again. "Have you ever listened to yourself say a word?"

"It's like thinking about breathing."

"Yes! It's just like that. When I talk, I can get to a point sometimes where I can see my sentences form in front of me. As if they're real things. It's like biting the words as they come out of my mouth. And then I forget to keep going and the words become sounds again."

"Have you ever laid in bed and thought about the act of falling asleep?"

"Thinking about blinking."

"Chewing your pot roast."

"Thinking about thinking."

"You hold your hand over a fire, thinking about how you hold it there."

"It's everywhere," he said. "Words, breathing, walking. The things we control and never consider. Isn't that funny?"

This was my fifth documentary with Colin. The first was on fracking, in a light political mode, Oscar-nominated, well ahead of the *Gasland* series. His notoriety is based largely on his prescience. In the late nineties, he did a short on the threat of bin Laden, and soon after Bush's reelection he did a feature length on housing bubbles, complex banking issues, deregulation, and the inevitable crash.

At the hooligan bar, Colin told me, "The tramplings are going to get worse. It's been two months since AT&T, but more will come. Then more, then more. School shootings worked the same way. First it was Columbine, then everywhere."

They all liked to make curious claims about the nature of time and fate.

Colin would have no memory of this premonition. This is the life of the prescient: they light us a path of lanterns, then cut deeper into the fog. I should have recorded what Colin said in that Glasgow bar, so I could play it again and again for him and eventually he would see how right he was.

· · ·

Attaching myself to Colin led to more consistently lucrative gigs. Sound work finally expanded my savings, and, using this new money, my wife and I moved with our two sons from New York City to a house in Danbury, Connecticut. We enjoyed paying the mortgage and bills at first, but as with movie making, surprise expenditures always arise. Last summer, our youngest turned three, and he still barely speaks a word. His ears have been checked and are working fine. We've spent thousands on specialists, doctors, and quasi-doctors, and will continue to until we hear the sound of his voice. I told my wife he appears brilliant in other ways, a doodler of uncommon talent, a spry and adept tumbler. He will be a dancer, I said, a choreographer of extraordinary merit, Nijinsky's reincarnation. Lessons to begin on his fourth birthday, no matter the cost.

Colin and I grew closer while shooting *Modern Tramplings*. He directed the crew when he needed to direct, but otherwise he spoke mainly to me. He seemed to get some toddler-ish joy in showily favoring my company. During our last day at Ibrox, I told him about my son's speech issues.

"Don't worry about him," Colin said, waving his Gatorade in the air. "Haven't I told you I spoke gibberish until I was five?" I thought about what that meant for my son: Colin had struggled with speech and look who he became. "I spoke caveman gibberish. My parents never thought to record me but they do great impressions if you ask."

"Do you understand what they're saying?"

"It's funny, my last visit I swore I heard something in their impressions. So when I was alone that night, I tried to speak the way I did when I was a kid. I tried not to think, just say, say, say. I tried to enter this primal state of speaking. I went to the basement, turned off the lights, and spoke gibberish to the walls. Isn't that funny?"

"But after so long, was your grammar all off?"

"Funny guy," he said. "I'm going to tell you something. It got real primal. It was like a coming home. Those religious people who speak in tongues? There's something there. I should look it up."

• • •

We interviewed tramplers, trampling survivors, friends, family, observers from afar, ballplayers, architects, building code enforcers, event planners, and so on. They all liked to make curious claims about the nature of time and fate. The tramplings, to them, were the result of long-working coincidences. They talked about life vectors, helixes spinning and merging in the dark, predetermination on the scale of an arcing universe. I understood the impulse to think this way, and so did Colin, who goaded them into these odd statements. A trampling is a tragedy, but it is also an embarrassment. For those involved, how better to analyze it than at the level of planets and asteroid belts? How better to sweeten their shame than by examining the shifts of tectonic plates, the rise and fall of empires, and how the past led them there?

• • •

Modern Tramplings would be long, a two-parter, East and West, or old and modern. Colin said he was doing it for Netflix.

"Everything is for Netflix now," he said. "It's about algorithms and the math of choice. Star ratings, cast connections, recommended for Colin. You liked that Werner Herzog—how about *Modern Tramplings*? But the idea is to hit everything. You like *Friends*, so how about *Modern Tramplings*? *A Streetcar Named Desire*, same thing. The future is in algorithms. Amazon, Goodreads, Urbanspoon. You have to Kevin Bacon it, maximize the connections. And let's get Kevin to narrate this."

I wondered if Colin meant *Modern Tramplings* was literally Netflix-funded. My bank statements were no clue—the deposits came from a check-paying company in Delaware, and once in an envelope of cash directly from Colin. But as long as he led the way, I didn't care where the money came from.

• • •

Colin kept a supermarket bag filled with cheap notebooks, a new habit. Throughout the day he would take them out either to create an entry or to refer to one. He allowed me to read them whenever I liked, an intimacy I took advantage of often on planes and buses. Most of the entries were cryptic observations of everyday life. I read one on how different pizza joints serve slices: on one or two disposable plates; on a tray; in a paper bag; or all three—on a plate in a bag on a tray. After our conversation about my son and Colin's childhood, I read one on speech patterns in feral children: he had been researching on the sly. Another was on the body language of shoppers and vendors. The entries were also a small explanation of his increasingly associative chatter.

"Bollywood," he said. "Troupes of dancers climbing into frame. A square of men and a square of women dancing on a hillside. I've never sat through a Bollywood movie, but there's something to the dance scenes. The crowds spilling off the edge of the screen, implying more. The colors everywhere. The gold chains and flying cloth. This is why I want to go to India."

If I'd known then how *Modern Tramplings* would change him, I would have interpreted his focus on India as more than the curiously shifting attention of a genius. But some things are impossible to foresee, and even Colin would have lacked insight at the time. From the outset, we both believed that he would spin the history of tramplings into effortless art. In truth, the tour and India would be something like watching Beethoven, unaware his ears are being paralyzed part by part until a horse soundlessly passes, or a door closes without a click, as suddenly he knows that genius realized can rapidly become genius lost.

Before Colin became a director he was a garbageman in Pennsylvania, where he lived with his parents until he was almost thirty. His first documentary was a short on garbage politics: where garbage goes after it's collected, how dump sites are chosen, and who wants those locations changed. He did it with a camcorder, as a fun thing for his garbage buddies. It was good enough to get him into Tisch, and twenty years later we began *Modern Tramplings*. His life has been pauper to prince, but despite his success he still lives in the cheap Brooklyn apartment he rented while at NYU, either by ascetic choice or simple necessity. On shoots, Colin bleeds money, but it's impossible to know if it's his. I've never seen his apartment—it may be filled with nice things, but I've always imagined it with cinder-block tables, a rumpled futon, an empty fridge, the type of place that in a hundred years they'll see how he lived and say we didn't appreciate him.

> **Perhaps his jocular waffling was evidence he was already questioning his talent.**

• • •

Every few days Colin and I edited interviews. I'd bring them organized in Pro Tools so they could be nimbly retrieved. Colin worked fast, shouting commands: cut, trash, reattach, rewind, exhume. I liked the pace. I liked even better when he slowed to discuss macro-level sound for the film's final trajectory. That is when I'd typically mine him for B-roll ideas, but I struggled to pinpoint his vision for *Modern Tramplings*. Sometimes he described interior shots: eyeball close-ups, fearful panting over a black screen. Other times I thought he'd go full Ron Fricke, with space-high time lapses of surging crowds. When I confessed my confusion, he laughed. "You're right. Where is my mind on this one? I should be certain by now."

Perhaps his jocular waffling was evidence he was already questioning his talent. Or maybe his eagerness for distraction was evidence enough. During one of our cutting sessions, my wife called, and Colin took the phone. He wanted her perspective on our son's lack of speech and to test the strength of his new research. He already employed arrow-precise vocabulary to explain reduplicated babble and the *schwa* sound's evolution. I should have been concerned that he so quickly leapt from *Modern*

Tramplings talk, but instead I was envious and somehow relieved that Colin could seemingly nurture so many preoccupations.

"Have you met a Pentecostal?" he said to her. "No? Let me tell you about glossolalia."

. . .

We interviewed people at the death sites, wandered through the haunt zones as they described the smells of a trampling, the strangled shouts of the dying. I tried not to imagine the scenes, but in my headphones I found this impossible. I need the volume high so I can catch sound issues. Sometimes, despite the wind guard, a mic still overloads. Sometimes, city sounds leap off a building and into my boom mic, and if I don't hear them, they'll reappear sneakily in postproduction, months later. So I turned up my headphones, asked people to repeat a sentence, and listened to their stories. The beautiful blue sky the day of the trampling, the joy in the air, those ironic banalities we all like to mention, the new beginnings, the cancelled birthday parties, as loud as shouts in my headphones, the recently graduated, the recently married, the recently divorced. It would be funny, they said, if it wasn't so terrible.

The day after North Attleboro, another trampling. Texas, near the border. Car race, pileup, panic.

. . .

Our first morning in Duisburg, Germany, a misting rain. We were at the site of the Love Parade disaster, twenty-one dead, over five hundred injured in a concert rush. Our interview subject was late, so to fill time I recorded footfalls on wet pavement. This is when we heard the news about North Attleboro, Massachusetts: one dead, fifteen injured at a Target, during the Black Friday blowout. I thought about my family, of course, but more pressing was Colin's prediction that America was entering a cycle of tramplings. I tried to be quietly rational. The incident was isolated, I thought, and we should have expected it on Black Friday.

I ducked away to call my wife anyway. She had already left a voice mail.

"I thought you'd worry about the trampling, so I called. We're fine, of course. Normal morning here: the boys wanted mac 'n' cheese. But the people at Stop and Shop—everyone was walking slowly, gently putting things in their carts. They excused themselves, and when they put things back on the shelves, they arranged them just so, as if they worked there. I could only do the same. There was nothing else I could do."

. . .

The day after North Attleboro, another trampling. Texas, near the border. Car race, pileup, panic. Three dead, twelve injured. A week later, while filming in Minsk, there were two tramplings on the same bleak Saturday. Orlando, Florida: five, eight. Then Macon, Georgia: seven, twenty-one. Overseas, we refreshed Huffpost, Slate, Yahoo News, BBC, Fox News, Drudge Report, the best and worst: anything. Though the incidents were accelerating, I tried to believe they were still isolated, and portended nothing. When we were alone, I told Colin that there was the grand floating cosmos to consider, time immemorial, as they say, the earth as a rune-carved sphere, shifting on a folded plane.

. . .

At night I tended to my field pack, cleaning out dirt with hotel Q-tips. I muted the TV and listened to the day's recordings, combing them for errors and lapses in fidelity. Sometimes Colin would enter unannounced and watch the silent TV—always tuned to a local channel—with me, and he would write an occasional note in a fluorescent, dollar-store notebook. It was on these occasions, after Orlando and Macon, that I first truly noticed the change in his demeanor. Where once he was content to poke fun at the low-rent broadcasts, now he saw the news jockeys, the fluff-piece interviewees, the menial local crooks as proof of some greater human failing.

"How can we control ourselves?" he said, eyes on the screen. "Should we even try?"

It soon became plain that *Modern Tramplings* was affecting him more deeply than his other documentaries. Work-mode Colin had always been a joy to watch, expedient in film making, adaptive, an unparalleled interviewer—he could make tyrants weep. After the new surge of tramplings, he began excusing himself during interviews, his face in a state of acute confusion. When he returned, he'd ask softball questions regarding location, weather, feelings before, during, and after the trampling. Usually, he would regain his composure before long. Checking the rolls at night, I could hear his voice change as he collected himself. I felt sorry for him when he was in the room with me—he didn't know I was analyzing his strange emotions. If I were to have asked him about it, I wouldn't have received an answer, so I left it alone. Nor did I prod him about his research on language and speech. That once-intense curiosity had all but evaporated from him. When we went out to dinner, I instead talked about sound theory, Ben Burtt's best work, my ideas for the final cut of *Modern Tramplings*. But Colin had again started abandoning me at restaurants to finish my meal alone, and not in the breezy way I was used to. Sometimes he would even forget to pay. He seemed overwhelmed by something, as if in need of a quick and quiet escape. At the time, I thought he was beginning to fear crowded places, narrow doorways, dumb circumstances, just like the rest of us. That was likely correct, but Colin would demand greater accuracy: he was haunted because he could no longer make sense of these fears.

. . .

Victoria Hall, 1883, Sunderland. Children rushing to collect a prize, inward opening door, 183 dead on the stairs. Water Festival, 2010, Phnom Penh. Crowded bridge, pushing, electrocution: 347, over 700. Four thousand dead in China, seeking cover from Japanese bombing, Chongqing, 1941. Hajj pilgrims in Mecca: 1,426 in 1990; 270 in 1994; 118 in 1998 . . .

One night, trying to sleep, I thought about these numbers we toss around. Shamefully, my mind turned to the math of disasters. There are codes in how we speak of the dead and injured, locked in their gruesome statistics. Perhaps it is best to think of it as an algorithm, I thought. It's about proximity, fear levels, history, and the dumbness of the situation. North Attleboro was so close to my family, so shouldn't the event have been newsworthy, foreboding, grand? Four thousand dead in China, and yet I found myself unmoved by the large number. Because aren't we always searching for records? The most dead, the most injured. Four thousand is impressive—it would be a shame if the number were lower. Algorithms, equivalencies. The language is in the numbers.

. . .

Arriving at our Moscow hotel, I realized I'd left my batteries and two microphones on a bench near airport customs. Colin's first interview was three hours later. I took a taxi to the airport, where staff couldn't produce my gear. It had either been stolen or permanently confiscated. Outside, I stood near a garbage can, waiting to puke. I wasted my hours rushing around Moscow, looking for equipment I could scarcely afford. Shops were closed, and shopkeepers were unhelpful. I had never been so careless before. I had witnessed many Colin tirades, but never absorbed one. Shaken, I returned to the hotel, where, in the lobby, the production assistant told me the shoot was cancelled. There had been a trampling in Pennsylvania near Colin's parents' home, and he wouldn't leave his room.

The production assistant was ready to contact the producers, but I talked her down. My wife had added another speech therapist to our son's schedule. I couldn't risk yanked funding. I told the production assistant that Colin would return invigorated the next day and spur us into making up time, that a day off would improve

It's about proximity, fear levels, history, and the dumbness of the situation.

the dollar-to-work ratio. She eventually believed me, though I wasn't sure I believed myself. She even gave me some incidental cash to replace my lost equipment. By the next morning, I was filling the B-roll with Russian wild sound.

· · ·

Malls, bar mitzvahs, schools. Masonic temples, convention centers, festivals. In a way, the tramplings began to feel the same. Place, number, number. Tucson, Kalamazoo, Missoula. Three, thirteen; twelve, forty-seven; six, twenty. Instead of being triggered by singular events, these tramplings seemed triggered by each other, by the fear of a trampling itself: the more that fear grew, the more likely another would occur. The production assistant wanted us to return to America to tape what was happening there: the movie should be about American tramplings. Colin would have none of it. He still needed to see India.

"Something has occurred to me," Colin said in my hotel bedroom. "The near misses, the almost involved. Take the Montana trampling. My uncle used to live in Missoula, an hour away. Take Texas, at the derby. I have been to derbies. I could have been trampled. Don't we all think this way? Think 9/11. You lived in New York then. Think of the people you knew outside the city, the hours they waited to hear your voice. In a way, it was them roaming the city, covered in white dust. North Attleboro isn't far from Danbury. What did you think when the trampling occurred? You thought about your family. Perhaps they went to Boston for a Thanksgiving trip, then stopped for Black Friday shopping on the ride back. It's so human to think this way, but no one admits to it—even you. We make the tramplings occur everywhere. We want to be involved. We want to collapse on strangers in the streets and tell them what we've lost."

> As with Rome, centuries from now, knowing better, they will say America had it coming.

I realized that through this abstraction he was asking me for consolation about the Pennsylvania trampling, which I tried to give him by explaining my thoughts on the algorithms of tragedy. I expected him to embrace the concept and fill the gaps in my thinking, but he didn't respond. Looking to fill the air, I said, "But I'm talking about history. What is there to say about what's happening now?"

He looked at me a while, then said, "I don't know." And because we had worked so closely for so long, I could detect a different fear in Colin's tone: his confidence in delivering on *Modern Tramplings* was being sapped.

We had an interview that afternoon, and, pitying him, I tried to help. I offered to run the interview in his stead, to allow him time alone. I told him that after five documentaries, I knew how he questioned. But I had miscalculated: he was not ready to admit aloud the movement I knew inhabited his heart. He rejected my idea with a grin and a single, punched laugh, collected his notebooks, and left my hotel room. Later we cancelled the interview anyway. Colin had melted into the Moscow crowds and we didn't know when he would return.

. . .

Three days later, Sarnia, Canada, a border town on Michigan's thumb. Two, ten. It didn't matter the circumstances, the historic energies, the Triassic beginnings. The border had been crossed.

We were filming in Jakarta—something about a boxing match. The streets were acrawl with people, and, with closed eyes, I heard only the noise of death. After the shoot, I kept Colin out of my hotel room. Twice he knocked heartily, but I didn't trust him anymore to guide me through my fears: it seemed he couldn't guide himself. I closed the drapes and lay on the bed. The death sounds fell through the thin hotel walls. Once you've decided to listen, they will not leave you alone. How horrible it will be when my son finally speaks—when his voice blends into that noise.

Midnight approached. We were flying to India the next day, and I needed sleep, but again I sat up thinking. Colin had been right—the shootings in America brought more shootings; the tramplings would bring more tramplings. This new phenomenon, I had thought, was purely American, self-made with our showy avarice, our dumb and selfish deaths. The pattern had secretly seemed deserved to me: as with Rome, centuries from now, knowing better, they will say America had it coming. But the map lines had been breached, and soon the American tramplings would be everywhere. In the hot, noisy hotel room, I imagined Toronto ablaze, its buildings toppling in slow, solid crashes. Mounties riding up the streets, chasing down the American death. I couldn't stop thinking this way. The thoughts had bitten down on my whirring mind. What is always present is always there, I thought, breathing deliberately. Freight ships in Fundy colliding in the ancient black water, and the peal of metal, prehistoric, terrifying, as waves push the ships over the barricades to slide dead along the docks. Nova Scotia, Halifax. The tramplings had already arrived, and they were riding the colored sky over the Atlantic to Iceland. It is not so far away if you look at a map. American tramplings, soon on every shore.

· · ·

India. We had come to film only three locations: Wai, Jodhpur, and Lucknow. Colin had mentioned constantly that India has had so many tramplings, we could have shot only there. From the start there were crowds. The airport, the train, the streets. We began in Lucknow, north, near Nepal. In 2004, the prime minister threw a large birthday party for an official. At the end, they gave out saris as favors. Twenty-one dead.

I had expected Colin to be newly energized by our arrival, enough so he could help me sort through the troubling thoughts I'd had in the Jakarta hotel. But he drew more into himself the farther we bored into India. He stood alone near a window on the train, his notebooks packed and forgotten, and remained in his hotel room once we arrived in the late afternoon. Our bank deposits were two days late. I was worried—I didn't know how long I could continue if payments were delayed. But I also knew that Colin could still strangle money from a giant like Netflix, if that was where the money was from. To stay productive, the cameraman and I toured Lucknow and filled our B-rolls, he with crowd shots, vendors with towers of sculpted spices, food carts burping fiery exhaust, and I with sounds of motorbikes, food queues, and auto-rickshaws.

When I returned, I found Colin's door open. His room was unusually tidy—aside from stacking his suitcases on the luggage rack, Colin hadn't touched a thing. He was on the balcony, looking over a square of city, and he invited me to join him. We were on the fifth floor. The sun was beginning to set when room service brought our Kingfishers. We leaned on the white railing like frat boys, holding the beers by their lips. I began to tell him about my walk through Lucknow, but he stopped me. He pointed to the square below and narrated what he saw. A man hauling his steam cart through the street, he said. A woman folding her bright saris. There is a man pulling down the metal security doors of a gas station. Between each observation, he paused as if stunned these moments weren't spilling into catastrophe. He said he had been watching the street all day, the weaving traffic, the near collisions, the horn blasts of commuters.

Then, from far off, came a pack of kids on bikes, dozens of them pedaling up the dusty street. Colin stopped talking, and we watched the kids ride. They were going fast, butts off their seats so they could lean all their weight on the pedals, rocking their bikes side to side for leverage. The kids were riding so close to each other that from the hotel balcony it seemed impossible their wheels weren't colliding. The closer they came, the faster they appeared to be moving, the more certain it looked that two of their brightly spinning wheels would clip, and the kids would all fall atop one another in a metal sprawl, a pile of kids and bike parts. A man wandered across the road. A car pulled out in front of the kids. A piece of broken curb jutted into the road. And then at the edge of the pack a boy flew over his handlebars, hands out, yelling as he landed safely on his knees, skidding a little on the pavement as his bike leaped from behind him, twirled in the air above him, and bounced down the street. The other kids rode on unaffected, and the boy rose immediately from the ground, grabbed his bike from traffic, and followed his friends as they disappeared around a curve.

Colin and I stared at the space where the kid had landed. Cars passed over it, and still we stared, not speaking. It felt as if we were waiting for some new event to explode out of that space and hand us the tragedy we had expected.

Eventually, Colin slumped onto a deck chair, his face blasted by the new colors of India. He looked as if he wanted to say something. I waited for him to deliver a screen-ready sum-up of everything we'd seen from Cincinnati to Lucknow, a voice-over I'd record to ease his audience into understanding.

I watched the street again, and began imagining my son's life on an arc like Colin's—from mute childhood to savant dancer, a sculpture of living movement, until the instant the limit of his genius is tested. If Picasso had lost a single eye and with it the sense of perspective he'd worked his life to undermine, would he, like Beethoven, have recovered? Or would he have succumbed like Nijinsky?

Colin said nothing. He entered his room, set his half-empty beer on the nightstand. He turned off the lights. 🔷

GRATEFUL DEAD TAPES

Even though we've already been dead,
in a secondhand store in Missoula
I found two trays of Grateful Dead tapes,
concerts bound in the stasis of cassette,
their plastic cases scarred and cracked
like old scuba goggles, some with the delicate
peg that lets the door swing open,
broken, maybe falling from a van's sliding
door to bright, cold pavement.
The homemade trays that held them were scrap
lumber joined by nail and glue that beaded
where slot met frame, the wood pen-pitted
like a history class desk, scar and doodle
against natural grain. A card insert scrawled
set list and stadium, but not the name of the owner
who let go the songs inside them, myth and rapture.
Could be no tragedy made the tapes secondhand
greater than the owner lost presence in their interest.
Used to listen to them, he might say,
the way you adjust to walking past a cemetery.
I love him, or her, who collected and cared
for these happenings, though the Dead's
not really my bag. I follow other melodies
and injured visions, draw my cider

from another press, lava in a lesser form.
I saw them once, summer of '95 at RFK.
with my friend Jax. It was terrible,
a lot of twentieth-century business coming due
at once. Bob Dylan opened, unintelligible
and sleepy as if reaching from the frost
to make known "in life I was Bob Dylan."
The Dead would play five more stands:
Auburn Hills, Pittsburgh, Noblesville,
Maryland Heights, Chicago, then done,
those last shows, autobiographies of indulgence.
Lightning struck a tree in the RFK parking lot.
I was weirded out and we left early.
The show was taped; every note is taped.
You can hear it forever at archive.org.
In my greatest period of disorientation
the Dead, like death, seemed best avoided.
Yet I was the sort who might admit
a simplifying affection like the Dead.
I remember, coming down in a cornfield

near a creek at dawn, talking it out with Jason
whether those trees were weird, or that
weirdness merely took the form of trees,
and every woman I pursued
had a pet cat that made me sneeze.
They liked either the Dead or Neil
Diamond. Yet I would persevere,
like one with a disorder, hanging
in the doorway to their petite kitchens
while they ground coffee, or searched
the crisper for a roommate's hidden beer.
I was trying to become more elaborate.
I knew I was too simple, and still am, ask
anyone about pleasure's light opera
and the children's music of the first kiss,
the hair metal of the second. And now
I play the Dead around the house.
It's children's music. We play operettas,
Pinafore, *Penzance*, for the same reasons,
because they are kind and almost meaningless.

I make few claims for poetry.
If a line lasts, it's not the poet's fault
or the paper that carries it forward,
rather an awkward chance,
like the wrench anthologized on its rack
or smudges on the yellow phone
in the thrift shop far from anywhere.
I didn't buy the tapes, or have yet to.
The price isn't marked, the clerk's busy.
I've kept only what marriage and child need
and a few books and held-back objects,
metal or paper, letters from old loves,
because letters are antique, and for
the limestone antiquity of those affections.

DOWNSTREAM

If you cook a pig in a roasting box
you might use a *caja china*, translated
usually as "magic box" instead of "Chinese
box," with China, the middle kingdom,
Caribbean slang (I'm told) for magic,
even the kind that broils a whole pig from above.
My friend Jeremy has one and we eat the proceeds
while listening to the '70s soft rock he collects,
although he's not a connoisseur of novelty,
as twilight presses down the monkey-puzzle tree
across the alley, *Araucaria araucana*,
the least sad tree ever grown. Jeremy grows
a winter beard. The monkey-puzzle, meanwhile,
is evergreen. I've never been to China or Cuba.
Trees are songs. Aside from "Ghostbusters,"
the saddest song ever written is "Kung Fu Fighting,"
sadder even than Orpheus on the hollow ground
after almost rescuing the woman he loves, after
having seen her, spoken to her in the shadows.
Had Orpheus learned kung fu he might have fought
the raving ones, who sent his head downriver
singing, but if the story is true, which it sort of is,
lyric poetry would never have washed ashore.
Carl Douglas, from Jamaica, recorded his chinoiserie

in ten minutes, an afterthought to a grueling session
being serious about a song nobody remembers.
Of course it has the oriental riff's pentatonic
racist baloney that signals "Asian," as Asian
as *la caja china*. What I've embarked on
in my forties is a verse that follows the rules
set by David Lynch in an episode of *Louie*
for hosting a late-night talk show: "First,
look 'em in the eye and speak from the heart.
And you gotta go away to come back,
and if someone asks you to keep a secret,
the secret is a lie." Presto: a hermeneutics
of confessional poetry. *Confessional*'s a term
like *magic realism*, long dead to the writers,
but high school teachers (whose brigades
once included a less-gray me) can still play
these instruments, along with "what does
this poem mean" & "what's it about?"
It's all a big mess, like an acre-wide tire fire
tended by tire fire specialists, to whom the fire
is matched only in beauty by the rubber
burning beneath, palisades of red spectra,
which merge and combine like harmonic notes,
egg-yolk-yellow riffs, orange motifs, then magenta.

And smoke converting past into future. The past
is what "Kung Fu Fighting" is about, what it means.
In the song, everyone was fighting, they no longer are.
Perhaps there is nothing now worth fighting about,
in any kind of fu. Like most riffs of the past,
it's racist in a way the present can see, which adds
sadness. I'm not beyond the future's conclusions,
those brutish future spirits who will hunt down
my intentions wherever I hide them from myself.
"Those cats were fast as lightning," Carl Douglas sings.
Those cats, in other words, are no longer lightning-fast.
Light is a meaningless measurement of their speed.
They are at best normal-fast; at worst, long since
slipped into the crematory of their own tire fires.
So warm. I can smell them from here, the other side.
When I listen to the same radio station for long,
say, a paint-spattered boom box hanging by a wire
beside the factory's time clock, or what the office pipes in.
Heard twice the same day, songs may lead to uneasy thoughts.
That second hearing—it's the feel of a cold coming on,
the blues, or desire, not the musical blues but the unspoken
and unwanted delicious, erotic but unfuckable blues.
The way things arrive! Storms and quakes, for example,
begin invisibly, but to one who is on their wavelength,
like the waves of a radio station, change is a sad song

punching inches ahead by the breath of waves.
A puff. A haze around the invisible fence.
Perplexed and wounded, at certain hours
I long to become animal or plant matter,
and if once it was a weasel writhing
measures along the Bitterroot, or a pond
bending flower or photogenic red maple,
at other times a monster, rippling in the dark,
or my own spectre, trying to hide the past,
or my phantom, trying to reveal it.
Written in haste by Ray Parker Jr. for the film,
the subject of "Ghostbusters" is ghosts,
so already gloom. Yes and no, the refrain's
double negative, reminds me I'm alert to fear,
and true, the ghost idea does and doesn't
scare me. I'm never sure. Reasons for dialing
begin with strangeness in the neighborhood,
things bad that don't look good, and then widen
to an invisible man sleeping in your bed,
meaning perhaps that he might as well
be invisible, or it is the bed retaining
a body's impress, lover gone to shadow,
Eurydice's absence driving Orpheus down.
You have to go away to come back, I've heard.
The last reason to call is if you're all alone.

THE PRANKSTER AND
THE PROFESSOR

David Gessner

One throbbed while the other thought

It began the day I was almost electrocuted by the novelist, poet, and nature writer Wendell Berry. If you don't know who Wendell Berry is, suffice it to say that he is a demigod in the nature writing firmament, but for a demigod he was quite friendly, refilling my iced tea and offering me crackers and laughing at my jokes. I may have been deluding myself, but he seemed to actually like me.

We had been sitting around Wendell's kitchen table—he insisted I call him Wendell, though I was having a hard time with it—talking about—what else?—literature.

The high point came when he mentioned the importance of water for our country's future, and I began to clumsily quote Robert Frost's poem "Directive"—getting some of the words wrong but getting the gist of the first line or two, which go "Back out of this all now too much for us/Back in a time made simple by the loss"—and then Wendell took over and, in a kind of Southern lilting baritone, quoted the entire rest of the poem from memory. I joined in for the last two lines, as if it were a sing-along: "Here are your waters and your watering place. / Drink and be whole again beyond confusion."

This was literary nirvana, of course, but there were also practical matters to attend to. It was a one-hundred-degree day in early July but by midafternoon the world outside the kitchen window had darkened and it started to sound as if some giant were ripping apart the fabric of the sky. Wendell interrupted our highfalutin talk to say he had to take Maggie, his border collie, to the barn to get the sheep in, and he invited me along. We climbed into his truck and drove to the barn with Maggie in the truck's bed and I stared down at the Kentucky River and at the land along its banks that Wendell had been farming for close to sixty years. When we arrived at the barn, Wendell asked me to hold open the metal gate, but then, glancing up at the lightning, said, "On second thought, you better not."

I should back up and explain how I happened to be at Wendell Berry's farm in the first place. A year before, in the fall of 2011, I had set out to write a book that would braid together the lives of the writers Edward Abbey and Wallace Stegner. The idea was to learn everything I could about Abbey and Stegner and then launch myself on a trip to the places that mattered most to the two men, while creating a kind of woven biography. Since both of them were dead, I would have to rely on people who had known them, and Wendell had been a classmate and defender of Abbey's, and a student of Stegner's. And since I would start my trip from my home in North Carolina and head west to the places where Abbey and Stegner lived,

Wendell's Kentucky farm was a logical first stop.

But a funny thing happened at the kitchen table that morning. We talked about Abbey and Stegner plenty, sure, and Wendell described the many ways that Stegner had influenced him. But another name kept barging into the conversation like an uninvited guest. For a good hour (I have the tape, so I know), we talked not about the men I'd come to learn about, but about another classmate of Wendell's, one I hadn't really thought about in years and one whom, frankly, I wasn't that interested in at first. Like most people, I knew Ken Kesey as the author of *One Flew Over the Cuckoo's Nest* and the subject of Tom Wolfe's *The Electric Kool-Aid Acid Test*. I'd developed a kind of mental CliffsNotes summary of his career, the way we do with writers whom we don't delve that deeply into, and my notes went like this: early success, leader of the hippie group the Merry Pranksters, lots of LSD, later burnout. It's true I had loved Wolfe's book, but the man at its center—not so much. I'd even seen Kesey give a reading sometime back around 1992 and he had come off as dull and dated, thick of body and seemingly of mind, uncomplicated and unsubtle and straining to still be groovy.

The Kesey that Wendell described, however, was a different sort of animal.

"He didn't like to drive in non-convertibles because they cramped his aura," Wendell said with a laugh. But if Kesey was eccentric and wild, he was also compassionate. Wendell told me a story about arriving at Kesey's house in Oregon, exhausted after a cross-country trip, to find everyone sitting in a circle, passing around a joint. What impressed Wendell was how solicitous Kesey was, understanding Wendell's exhaustion and his desire not to join in, and so ushering him off to a well-made bed in the guest room.

Wendell pointed out a similarity between Kesey and Stegner.

"Ken stayed married to the same woman his whole life," he said. "He was a curiously devoted man."

This did not sound like the Kesey I'd seen or the one I remembered from Wolfe's pages, the one who took acid and fooled around in the woods with a fellow Merry Prankster called Mountain Girl while back at the house his wife, Faye, made cookies and raised their three children. The one who rejected tradition and embraced LSD, and the one who would come to represent, in Stegner's mind, all that was wrong with the 1960s.

• • •

Books have plots, of course, but so too the writing of books: the creation of narrative follows its own narrative arc. I didn't know it that day at Wendell's, but that was the beginning of a significant subplot in the writing of my own book. Though Kesey would play only a minor role in the actual finished product, he lurked like a shadow, sometimes just out of sight, as I went about gathering material on the life of Wallace Stegner.

Stegner believed in tradition. On the surface, that sounds like a trite sentence. It isn't. Stegner grew up with a father who flouted the rules, and who often ditched his family as he went running off in search of a magic land that would become the title of one of Stegner's early novels, *The Big Rock Candy Mountain*. A big, strong, vital man who was never satisfied, always looking elsewhere, George Stegner seemed to his son to value imaginary riches over the well-being of his family, including the wife he abused and the little boy he bullied. To the son, the father embodied a type of Western character that Stegner would write about all his life, the "boomer," who searched for the quick strike whether in oil, gold, land, or tourism. In contrast to the boomer, Stegner idealized his mother as a "sticker," one who tried to settle, learn a place, and commit to it. These latter qualities comprised the platform from which Stegner both wrote and preached: commitment to place, respect for wild and human communities, responsibility for and to the land. Having grown up with a man who was the classic Western "rugged individualist," Stegner spent a lifetime debunking that myth.

In the face of his rootless past, Stegner deeply valued roots and the rooted.

The Kesey that Wendell described, however, was a different sort of animal.

Along with novels that won both the Pulitzer Prize and the National Book Award, he wrote histories and biographies, and extolled what he called "the historical imagination," the ability to think back in time, throwing off the prejudice of our own eras and seeing those trapped in their eras for who they were. Loyalty was another attribute that took on almost mystical importance: while his father was disloyal, Stegner stayed married to his wife, Mary, for almost sixty years, until the end of his life. At least one friendship ended because a friend was not equally loyal to his own spouse, a woman who was also Stegner's friend. He strove to be large; one of my favorite of his quotes is "Largeness is a lifelong matter." But if he lived a moral life he could not help but sometimes use the same standards to judge the lives of others. He was aware of this and tried to keep it in check but did not always succeed. During a visit to Stegner's former summer home in Vermont, I asked his son, Page, if Stegner could be intimidating. Page Stegner clearly loved and respected his father, and characterized their relationship as a good one, but he admitted it was sometimes challenging having a monument for a dad.

"It wasn't always easy growing up with a father who spoke the King's English," he said.

During our talk Wendell had called Stegner "a decided man."

While Stegner might have been "decided," Wendell's description of his teaching style, which matched other descriptions I'd heard, was that he was low-key, a great listener. But he could also be tough, and grew to be especially tough on Ken Kesey.

"It was like playing football under Vince Lombardi," Kesey would later say with more than a little admiration. Like Lombardi, Stegner did not tolerate bunk. In *The Uneasy Chair*, Stegner's biography of his friend, mentor, and fellow Western writer Bernard DeVoto, Stegner wrote: "He marshaled facts with great swiftness and made them into generalizations, and he discriminated among ideas with the positiveness of one discriminating between sound and rotten oranges." There was something of the same briskness, the same intellectual vigor and sweeping aside of the inessential, about Stegner. He was an unrepentant workaholic who delighted in crossing items off his lists, always working at the multiple tasks of writing, teaching, and environmental advocacy.

As the 1960s began, Stegner, now in his fifties, found himself at odds with some of the young mavericks in the program he'd founded, the Stanford Creative Writing Program, and notably with Kesey, who

As for Kesey, he had discovered a new world through LSD and had no use for the old world that Stegner represented.

later said of their split: "I took LSD and he stayed with Jack Daniel's; the line between us was drawn." But it wasn't the superficial differences that increasingly irritated Stegner. He believed that the hippie philosophy was essentially phony, a false and easy view of life that ignored its hard realities and responsibilities, and when he sorted through the fruit, he knew it to be a particularly rotten orange.

Kesey was a wrestler at the University of Oregon, a country guy with, as Wolfe famously put it, a "hell of a build," when he applied to the Stanford program. As it turned out, it was Edward Abbey, a student in the program at the time, who read the Oregonian's application, writing this comment on Kesey's novel about college sports: "Football has found its James Jones." Stegner read this comment, apparently found the work to his liking as well, and admitted Kesey.

But at Stanford Kesey didn't exactly follow a traditional route. Soon he was working at a psych ward while also volunteering at a local veterans hospital for an experiment, conducted by the CIA, that required him to take a series of drugs that included mushrooms, mescaline, and a then still legal but unknown drug that we now call LSD. At the same time, Kesey was submitting parts of a novel called *One Flew Over the Cuckoo's Nest* to his creative writing workshop with Stegner, a workshop in which Stegner stressed, as one of his great tenets, the importance of point of view. In fact, it was a breakthrough in point of view that elevated Kesey's novel above the ordinary, but that breakthrough came in a most un-Stegnerian fashion. While munching on peyote, Kesey created his Indian narrator, Chief Bromden. "It came from nowhere," he said later. "I didn't know any Indians." According to Wolfe, and to Kesey himself, many of the pages of the book were written under the influence of LSD, and though most of those pages were eventually thrown out, it seems obvious that the insights from the drug, combined with his job in the psych ward, gave Kesey an insider's look at madness.

While Stegner valued tradition and restraint, the star of Kesey's novel, Randle McMurphy, is the embodiment of rebellion. Who could be a more perfect symbol for the ascending '60s than McMurphy? And who could better represent all the things that Stegner was coming to despise about that rebellious decade?

As for Kesey, he had discovered a new world through LSD and had no use for the old world that Stegner represented. He soon kissed the institution of the university goodbye and took his show over the hill to his mountain retreat in La Honda, where he began his experiment in communal living with the Merry Pranksters, a kind of religious life with LSD as its central sacrament. He left Stanford even further behind when he and the other Pranksters climbed on their Day-Glo bus for a cross-country trip, with Kerouac's old sidekick Neal Cassady at the wheel. But even then his former teacher was not fully exorcised from Kesey's thoughts, and Kesey would later say in a *Paris Review* interview that Stegner may have played a part in the launching of that famous bus ride:

At one point, I read that he had said he found me to be ineducable. I had to stew for a long time over what Stegner didn't like about me and my friends. We were part of an exceptional group, there's no doubt about it. There was Bob Stone, Gurney Norman, Wendell Berry, Ken Babbs, and Larry McMurtry. All of us who were part of that group are still very much in contact; we all support each other's work. Stegner was the great force that brought us all together. He put together a program that ruled literature in California and, in some ways, the rest of the nation for a long time. Stegner had traveled across the Great Plains and reached the Pacific but, as far as he was concerned, that was far enough. Some of us didn't believe that it was far enough and when we went farther than that, he took issue with it, especially when it was not happening in the usual literary bailiwicks that he was accustomed to. I took LSD and he stayed with Jack Daniel's; the line between us was drawn. That was, as far as he was concerned, the edge of the continent, and he thought you were supposed to stop there. I was younger than he was and I didn't see any reason to stop, so I kept moving forward, as did many of my friends. Ever since then, I have felt impelled into the future by Wally, by his dislike of what I was doing, of what we were doing. That was the kiss of approval in some way. I liked him and I actually think that he liked me. It was just that we were on different sides of the fence. When the Pranksters got together and headed off on a bus to deal with the future of our synapses, we knew that Wally didn't like what we were doing and that was good enough for us.

• • •

I took the River Road along the Kentucky as I left Wendell's house. I remember being startled by what I at first thought was a smear of blood on the road. It turned out to be a dead cardinal. A little later a big deer, dark and tawny, ran in front of my car, crashing into the woods on the other side.

"I loved him but I never felt equal to him," Wendell said of Stegner. "We became friends but it took me a long time to call him anything but *Mr*. Stegner."

I knew what he meant. Two years of studying Stegner had done little to diminish my initial impression that he was a great writer and a good man, but he remained intimidating, even posthumously. When I interviewed Stegner's son and daughter-in-law they had referred to him as "Wally" and suggested I do the same. I couldn't bring myself to do it.

Before I left Wendell's, Kesey snuck into the conversation one last time:

"I got in between Stegner and Kesey," he told me. "I liked them both. What Stegner didn't understand about Kesey was how ambitious he was. They were of course alike in that way."

Wendell described a poetry reading he did at Stanford, an event that Stegner attended. He read, among other things, a poem called "Kentucky River Junction," which describes a visit that Kesey and fellow Prankster Ken Babbs paid to Wendell's house. "It was such a sweet meeting," Wendell said.

After the reading Stegner came up to him and said of the poems: "I liked them all but one."

When Kesey visited Stanford to read, Stegner refused to attend.

From Wendell's hometown of Port Royal I drove to Lexington, where I planned on interviewing Ed McClanahan, who had been Stegner's office mate in the '60s. This time I wasn't as surprised when Kesey barged into the conversation. McClanahan had been one of the original Merry Pranksters.

McClanahan was eighty years old at the time of our meeting but certainly didn't seem it. The bar where we met was loud and required if not yelling then good volume, and as we drank beers he proved up to the task. He told me that during his time, Stanford had been a stimulating environment and that at the beginning of the year, and sometimes during the year, Stegner would have the students up to his house on his then-secluded hilltop. He recalled a particularly stunning afternoon up at the Stegners' when he and the other members of

the workshop were having drinks out on the back patio in the late afternoon and someone looked up and noticed a hawk with a big rattlesnake in its talons circling above. While not every day could have been that dramatic, it occurred to me that those visits to the house on the hill must have been as stimulating for the students as the classes themselves. They got to experience a working writer's home with a studio out back and a book-lined living room, a place of the sort they might perhaps one day inhabit and a writer's life they might imagine one day leading.

McClanahan was one of the first to follow Kesey over the hill to his La Honda getaway, and was one of the first to take LSD, but he was not part of the cross-country trip in the bus named Further. "You're either on the bus or off the bus" is the refrain of Wolfe's *The Electric Kool-Aid Acid Test*, referring to those who got it and those who didn't. The great tragedy of McClanahan's life was that he was off the bus. By choice. In fact, he was there as the bus pulled away, a moment he has always regretted.

"I stood in Kesey's yard and waved goodbye," he told me. "And I've kicked myself ever since."

As we sipped beer, McClanahan described the origin of the conflict between Stegner and Kesey, an event at which he had a front-row seat.

"Stegner was a buttoned-down fellow," McClanahan said. "A very tightly controlled person. Which is not to say he was not a kind man."

According to McClanahan, the split between Kesey, the student, and Stegner, the teacher, began when Kesey gave an interview to Gordon Lish for the magazine *Genesis West.*

"In the interview Gordon asked him what his experience in the writing program had been like and Ken said he felt that Mr. Stegner—I imagine he was pretty respectful and might have called him 'Mr. Stegner'—had been too much lionized by his students and other people, and that it had gone to his head. And I don't know what the exact words were but the drift of it was that this had badly affected Stegner's writing in some way or other. A pretty thoughtless comment.

"Kesey felt bad about it. Felt it had been taken out of context. That's everybody's excuse these days, but it probably had been taken a little out of context. Gordon would do things like that. Ken felt awful. And he came to the office one day carrying a big red shiny apple. He brought it in there to see Stegner and Stegner wasn't in. But Dolly Kringle was there; she was the secretary, a kind of institution, and he left the apple with her. And when Mr. Stegner came in—you know I sometimes think I was there in the office when this happened. I think, but I'm not sure. I think I

was. But it may have been just what Dolly told me afterward. Anyway, Stegner came in and Dolly told him that Ken Kesey had been in and was very apologetic and that he left this big apple. I don't know what he did with the apple—threw it at Dolly?—but he wasn't in a forgiving mood. He just looked at Dolly without smiling and said: 'Well, he said it, didn't he?'

"It was pretty cold."

After that, Kesey came to represent for Stegner all that was wrong with the '60s: the drugs, the anarchy, the recklessness, the trashing of hard-won traditions. Over the next decade, "radical" was a word Stegner came to despise. He believed, along with his fellow hard-nosed realist, Samuel Johnson, that most of the cures for humanity are palliative, not radical. He had little patience for anything extreme. On more than one occasion he said that he disliked writing that "throbbed rather than thought."

• • •

One Flew Over the Cuckoo's Nest was published to nearly universal acclaim in 1962. Two years later Kesey published *Sometimes a Great Notion*, a sprawling novel about an Oregon logging family, and while this time the acclaim was less universal, it is considered by more than a few critics to be his

On more than one occasion he said that he disliked writing that "throbbed rather than thought."

greatest novel. After that, he effectively stopped writing for ten years and his later fiction and essay collections, published decades after the first two novels, do not hold up to his earlier work. The standard take is that his brain was fried. But what seems more relevant, and what Wolfe details in his book, is that Kesey had lost interest in the idea of sitting alone in a room and typing. When reading Wolfe's description of the magic bus trip today, with all the filming and taping of every moment, it is hard not to think of the Internet and iPhones and the fact that the Pranksters were decades ahead of their time. Wolfe makes the argument that the Pranksters virtually invented the '60s, from psychedelia to tie-dye to the font used on contemporary posters. But what Wolfe couldn't see, locked as he was in his time, was that they also invented, or at least anticipated, the future we now inhabit.

. . .

While doing research for my book I happened to run into John McChesney, a filmmaker who was making a documentary on the Western fracking boom. I asked him about his project and then he asked me about mine.

He laughed out loud when I told him.

"I lived in the cottage behind Stegner's house in the 1960s," he said.

"No fucking way," I said.

He then told me a story from that time. McChesney had been a student activist at Stanford, and was part of a group that occupied University Hall. It was pretty tense for a while, the police were called in, and it looked like the situation would turn violent, but the faculty senate granted the protesters amnesty and the students went home after two or three days.

"When I got home, Wally was sweeping off his patio. That was my regular job, part of my rent. He wouldn't look at me. But I did hear him mutter one phrase: 'Ruined a great university.'"

Stegner quit teaching at Stanford in 1971. Though he was, by almost all accounts, a great teacher, he showed some cracks by the end. He said this upon his retirement: "I am never going to miss teaching . . . I never gave it more than half my heart, the ventricle, say." Once he quit, he felt that for the first time in his life he was able to concentrate fully on individual projects. Over the next twenty-two years, until his death at eighty-four, he produced six books of nonfiction, including his underrated biography of Bernard DeVoto, and three of his best novels: *Crossing to Safety*, the National Book Award–winning *The Spectator Bird*, and the Pulitzer Prize–winning *Angle of Repose*.

Just as it had been for Kesey, and just as he had always advised his students, it was a breakthrough in point of view that elevated Stegner's later work. The first hints of where things would go showed as far back as 1952 with the creation of Joe Allston, the narrator of the short story "A Field Guide to Western Birds." Joe is a literary agent who has retired to his home in the California hills, where he lives with his wife, Ruth. More importantly, he is the prototype of the classic first-person old-man Stegnerian doppelgänger, what I came to call the "grumbling grandpa" narrators who are crucial to his later novels. Through his use of these exaggerated fictional stand-ins, Stegner created some of his best, and certainly most readable, fiction. Joe Allston came back for the novels *All the Little Live Things* and *The Spectator Bird*, and a similar, if less jokey, narrator named Larry Morgan took over for Stegner's last novel, *Crossing to Safety*. Both of these men are opinionated, gruff, and none too happy about the way the world has been hijacked by its at once softheaded and dogmatic young people. To the contemporary ear, there is an aw-shucks manner that takes some getting used to, particularly with the Joe Allston narrator, who has a little dash of by-golly Ronald Reagan jargon in his vocabulary (if not his politics). But all three protagonists have a barely disguised old-fashioned agenda. They embody continuance and rootedness, though they are not mere symbols of those qualities. These are novels, after all, not sermons, and the beauty of the books is that the old "decided" men who narrate them are actually full of uncertainty, anxiety, and questioning. Luckily, all of these men are also sharp, smart, and articulate, and it is the articulation of that uncertainty that brings the books alive.

Lyman Ward, the narrator of *Angle of Repose*, is a darker version of Joe Allston and Larry Morgan. He has reason to be dark: he is literally truncated, his legs amputated by the same doctor who has since run off with his wife. Meanwhile, his politically radical son doesn't think his father can take care of himself and hopes to put him in a nursing home. Stegner began this book at the height of his troubles with the young radicals who had "ruined" Stanford, and there is both some serious venting about the state of the rootless young and something close to conscious self-parody in the hippie-hating Ward. Tired of the shallow present, the narrator, a historian by trade, tunnels into the past, specifically into the lives of his pioneering Western grandparents, Oliver and Susan Ward. These excursions into the past are first presented as artifacts, the transcripts of letters. But they soon segue into a third-person re-creation of the past, dramatizing the lives and many moves of Susan and Oliver. In the course of empathizing with his grandparents and imagining their lives, the historian narrator becomes something else, something very close to a writer of fiction.

The Pulitzer-winning *Angle of Repose* is Stegner's greatest novel, but for our purposes it is worth dwelling on a lesser, earlier work, *All the Little Live Things*, which came out in 1967, a year before Wolfe's book launched Kesey to new heights of psychedelic fame. There is a character in that novel named Jim Peck, who lives in a tree house in the woods near the Allston/Stegner property and who spouts about free love and peace and who has followers who are drawn in by his raw charisma. He is a freeloader and "a fool," according to Allston, the type of Caliban character who throbs rather than thinks, and most scholars have seen him as a fictional representation of Kesey. Stegner denied this. His biographer, Philip Fradkin, writes that Stegner considered Kesey more dangerous than Peck and quotes him as saying that Kesey was "a person of more force than mind. I think Kesey is crazy as a coot, and dangerous, and rather special in his charismatic qualities, and with what was once a fairly big raw talent."

Even if Jim Peck is not based directly on Kesey, it stands to reason that parts of Kesey found their way into the various radical characters Stegner created during the '60s and '70s. As a writer it is natural to process one's own conflicts in one's imagination and on one's pages.

And what of Kesey turning Stegner into fiction?

Well, there was enough of a rift between the two men to lead at least one scholar to suggest that Kesey actually based Nurse Ratched, one of the most (if not the most) notorious authority figures in all of American literature, at least partly on the man running the program where he studied. Stanford professor and literary scholar Mark McGurl, whose book *The Program Era: Postwar Fiction and the Rise of Creative Writing* is a brilliant treatment of the rise of creative writing programs and their impact on postwar literature, writes: "It is hard to read

> They embody continuance and rootedness, though they are not mere symbols of those qualities.

about the bad behavior of McMurphy in the Group Meeting, his too evident disrespect for Nurse Ratched, without connecting it to Kesey's well-documented antagonism toward his teacher Wallace Stegner, whom, as John Daniel reports, Kesey saw as the 'epitome of economic staidness and convention' even as Stegner found Kesey 'irritatingly half-baked.'"

But wait a minute here. Nurse Stegner? Are we meant to imagine Stegner, white-maned novelist, environmental hero, and dean of Western writers, in a nurse's uniform and little hat, enforcing order on a group of patients in a psych ward? Perhaps it's a little easier to see Kesey, the Merry Prankster himself, in the role that Jack Nicholson later made famous (in a movie Kesey claimed to hate), the leering, jeering, sniggering Randall McMurphy, the great disrupter of the ward's peace and archenemy of the feared Big Nurse. And maybe in Kesey's mind this made some artistic sense: a crazy dance of authority and rebellion, Kesey trying to avoid the fate of his character, drugged and electroshocked into conformity, and Stegner trying to retain control of the institution he runs.

Malcolm Cowley was another teacher of Kesey's at Stanford, and he had this to say about *One Flew Over the Cuckoo's Nest*: "It's interesting how the judgments on that book divide along age lines." So too our reactions to Kesey and Stegner. I remember reading *The Electric Kool-Aid Acid Test* as a young man and being caught up in the wildness and charisma of the chief Prankster, and not long after that gobbling down some LSD of my own. But as I grew older, and especially as battles with mental illness became part of my family life, I began taking notes for an essay called "Some Words in Defense of Nurse Ratched." The piece had nothing to do with Stegner, at least not intentionally or directly, but was about the romantic and fuzzy picture the public seems to have of schizophrenia, as opposed to the tougher and more hard-eyed ideas that I had developed through personal experience.

. . .

As he grew older, Kesey, to his credit, came more fully to appreciate and understand Stegner, and in at least that one way he was perhaps his old teacher's moral superior: he was no grudge holder. If Stegner held grudges he was large in many other ways: he was a steady loyal friend, a great fighter for the environment and the underdog, a big thinker whose ideas have never been more relevant than in today's warming and overconnected world. As a man, he strove to overcome his own smallness and as a novelist he possessed empathy to an extreme degree, constantly entering the worlds of others, priding himself (for good reason) on his "ventriloquism," his ability to speak for others in his fiction. That's what made his inability to see Kesey's world striking. It wasn't like him.

So why did this empathy stop at Kesey's door? For one thing, bad timing. Bad timing that the generation Stegner encountered just as he entered later middle age reminded him in its looseness and lack of commitment of his bootlegger father. And suddenly here was this young star of this new generation, a big, charismatic, physically strong dreamer-schemer, a man who liked to break the law and the rules and who said to hell with the past, give me the future. A later model George Stegner, in other words.

It must have seemed to Stegner that the myth of the rugged individualist, whether in the form of a prankster or a cowboy, just wouldn't die. The costumes of hippies were just a new disguise for an old irresponsible type.

As for Kesey, rebelliousness was ingrained in his nature and who better to rebel against than the ultimate father figure, Stanford's very own Old Testament God?

In his essay "The Prankster Moves On," John Daniel, who knew both men, writes:

> The trouble between them, I think now, may have stemmed as much from their likeness as it did from their differences. Each made his way to literary fame from inauspicious beginnings in the rural West, and each arrived with an attitude stamped into his soul. Stegner's was: When you start with nothing you'd better work, work, work. Kesey's was: Watch out or high culture will suck out your life.

> There's validity to both.

As I get older I find myself more often on Stegner's side of the divide, and like him and his friend Bernard DeVoto, I find myself tossing aside the rotten oranges of soft and romantic thought. But just because the years have separated me from my own earlier experiences, I don't want to forget the energy I once drew from books both by and about Kesey.

I remember something that Wendell Berry said as we sat at the kitchen table on that hot July day.

"We all have our personal ecosystems," he told me. "An ecosystem is full of dependencies, and nothing in it knows what it is dependent on."

That made great sense to me then and still makes sense to me now. We never know what we are getting from others. If we are lucky, our reading and influences are like a vast underground root system, and about as easily deciphered. I know I could never map where most of what I have gotten has come from.

"The personality stuff isn't important in the end," Wendell said. "People die out of it. It goes away. There's nothing to it. The books and ideas remain."

In setting out to write my book, I had chosen Wallace Stegner as one of my subjects, at least in part because he was a great model, not only as a man but also for all that he had achieved in his older years. This seemed particularly relevant for someone like me, who had just crossed to the other side of fifty. But models are never so clear-cut. If my choice of Stegner was a conscious decision, my choice of Ken Kesey was not. He had, as was his habit, appeared unexpectedly, butting in, a Prankster till the end.

As it turned out, there was room at the party for both. While I cannot tell you exactly how they have acted on me, I do know they are each in their own way good company. Their old antagonisms long faded, something of them each still remains, and it is a something that I am deeply thankful for. These days Mr. Stegner and Mr. Kesey can mingle without acrimony, and they are there, waiting together, for those of us who would seek them out. 🜚

the bus

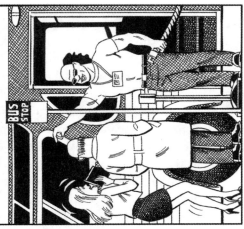
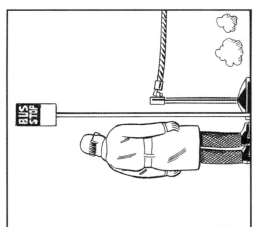
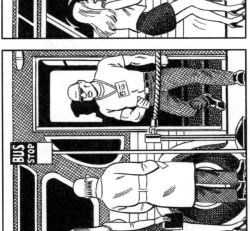
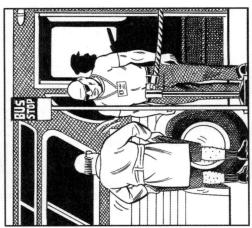
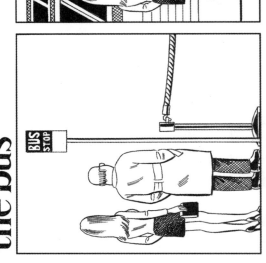

the bus

PAUL KIRCHNER

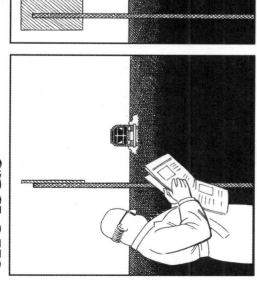
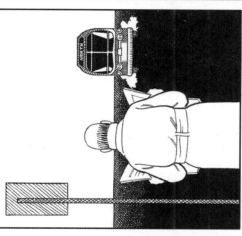
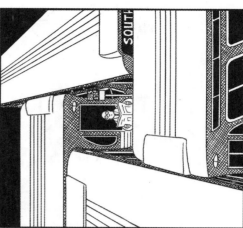
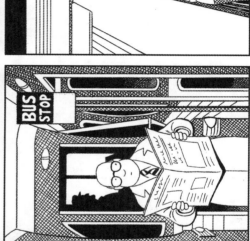

DUDEPOEM (BENEATH THE DUDE OF THE NO DUDE DUDE UP FROM MY MORNING BED)

A snake Though a snake
Is beautiful Obviously But a dude

I saw a coyote this morning And
Steve's in town So

Was Steve
The coyote

And Chris is pregnant
With friendship Or So he says

But that's A little weird
Isn't it

Dudes are so
Disappointing And

I am one. Maybe more
Dudes should read

How Should a Person Be
By Sheila Heti Which

is a book I read Halfway
But plan to go back

Someday soon Because that's
the Problem perhaps

The being And
The person

Dudes are persons
Sometimes Just shitty

I dream a future Not literally
When all dudes are good

Persons Fair and kind Loving
Not Like I love Oakland and have

Ever since *Operation*
Stackola dropped But purely

I do want dudes
To do their part And

To do my part
As a dude

To make everything
Chill for everyone

To sit on a bus
In such a way

As to make everyone feel
Welcome and comfortable

And respected And
Not in such a way

As to make anyone feel
Unloved. I believe

That humanity will
Reach toward Yes, yes

But first Dudes need to
Be quiet a moment

And stop being
Dick Simple

I don't have an idea
I'm just thinking

An osprey
Taking a siesta

In a purple field of Whatever
And so

A poem it must be
Cauliflower like

And full of
Love But

I am aware and
Do hate that I am

A dude
Talking dudeliness

It's rude Please forgive me Again
And I'm struggling now

To be a person So
I'll practice Breathing

And dancing with my hands
By Opening for the 1st time

Picasso's Tears by Wong May
Book beautiful

Like 2 buildings
Looking at each other She says

And listen to The death song
Of passing cars For

All I want to bring to the table
Is joy and love and

That's all I really wanted to say
Joy and Love Joy and Love

FICTION

Those Less
Fortunate

Jennifer S.
Davis

S arah wakes to her father perched on the edge of her bed. The music she plays to put herself to sleep each night—garage-punk lamentations she finds particularly comforting—is spilling from her earbuds onto her breasts. The bass burrows there, deep in her chest cavity, her heart lurching to catch the chorus's beat. Outside her bedroom window, the sun has yet to pink the horizon; the moon droops in the sky, a doleful, half-shut eye.

"I didn't want to wake you," her father says.

"Then why are you sitting there?" Sarah rolls over onto her stomach, her face pressed into her pillow. The smell of her breath—peach wine coolers and weed—is enough inspiration to flip back over. "Fuck *me*," Sarah says. She can feel her father flinch, the quiver of the mattress.

"Because we need to get going."

"Then you did want to wake me up. So just say that."

"I didn't *want* to wake you, but we *need* to go."

Before she can stop him, he tugs her ear twice, a forgotten ritual of affection. He seems at a loss after this gesture. "I guess we could pray together," he offers. "Everybody's always saying it helps." Outside of funerals and Christmas dinner, Sarah has never known her father to pray.

Sarah can hear the TV playing from the living room, the distorted roar of a crowd. She's seen all the videos often enough to know which of her brother's old game tapes is playing, that a grainy Sean is bursting across the screen right now, his right hand pumping the air with the football as he peers downfield for an open receiver.

"I saw the face of Jesus in my hamburger bun last night," Sarah says. "I'm all good for now."

"I'm trying here, Sarah." Her father sits quietly for a moment, his breathing labored, as if he's run a very long distance. Then he rallies. "Come on, this will make you feel better. It's important to remember folks less fortunate than us."

"There are people less fortunate than us?" Sarah says. "Now that's depressing."

He presses a quick kiss to her forehead and stands and leaves, turning on the light as he disappears down the hallway, past her brother's door, which is kept open, the dresser covered in an army of sports trophies, seamed little men clutching misshapen footballs in midthrow; past her parents' closed door, where her mother is sleeping, has been sleeping for several months now, and will be sleeping no matter when Sarah returns home today.

Sarah's father manages grounds maintenance at one of the golf courses on the lake, the reservoir that is the saving grace in their town, though only the locals who inherited property or bought lakefront lots decades ago can afford to enjoy it. Mostly, it belongs to weekenders. Everybody else lives on rural tracts outside the town limits, like Sarah's family does, or in the small town center, which, after her father punches an address into the GPS from a list on a torn slip of notebook paper, is where they head first.

> **Seven half-frozen Thanksgiving turkeys are secured carefully under a tarp in the bed of her father's truck.**

The narrow streets are nearly empty, a ridge of red just cleaving the bruise of clouds in the east. They pass the gas-station-turned-video-store-turned-laundromat-turned-Chinese-buffet. Her dad points it out, says, "We should try that new restaurant one of these days. You like Chinese?" and Sarah thinks that being with her father is like being on an awkward date with a nice boy you're really not that into.

Seven half-frozen Thanksgiving turkeys are secured carefully under a tarp in the bed of her father's truck. The plan—as her father explained it to her yesterday in a serious tone that let her know there was no escape from this day of daughter-father togetherness—is to drop off the turkeys at the homes of the guys on his crew at the golf course, then drive out to a buddy's land near Opelika to introduce Sarah to the pleasures of deer hunting.

When not working, her father usually looks like an older, heavier version of the country boys at her school: a snug Henley with low-slung jeans and a cap with a well-bent bill shading a slab of thick bangs. Today he's decked out in full camouflage, a fluorescent orange cap tugged low over his baggy eyes. The few days' growth of hair on his cheeks, mostly white, is brilliant against his tanned skin.

"These are good men," he is telling her now.

"Okay," Sarah says.

"They just made some bad choices, some missteps along the way. Most places won't hire them—hell, most places ain't hiring anybody in this economy—but I give a man a chance to show himself."

"Like what?" Sarah asks. "What kinds of bad choices?"

"Take your pick. There's a whole world of trouble out there."

Acid froths and burns in Sarah's throat. She grabs a bottle of Gatorade from the lunch cooler her father prepared and chugs the entire thing. Her swallows pound against the sea wall of her skull, and she thinks of Sean, what it must have sounded like when the doctor drilled a hole into her brother's head to release the pooling blood. A cranial burr hole, they'd called it, which Sarah thinks would make a sweet name for a band.

> A cranial burr hole, they'd called it, which Sarah thinks would make a sweet name for a band.

Her father casts a sidelong glance her way from under his cap. "You're being responsible with those friends of yours, right? You're not doing anything too stupid?"

Sarah's friends are new friends, a group of perpetually stoned teens who move with a sleepy languidness, as if their bodies battle some unseen resistance. Sarah, who'd always been a do-gooder, the kind of girl who ran the Toys for Tots campaign each Christmas, barely noticed these kids skulking the hallways of the school before this year, an almost invisible black-clad tribe who took her in with as much warmth and enthusiasm as they show for anything or anyone.

In part because it's a legitimate point and in part because he's annoying her, Sarah asks, "Don't you think it's too early to just show up at somebody's house?"

Her father grins, his front teeth stained from the cigarettes he sneaks when she and her mother are not around. "Who wouldn't wake up early for a free turkey?" Somehow, he looks sadder when he smiles.

They turn onto a street that borders the main town cemetery. The tiny wooden cottages are the sun-leached gray of driftwood. They park in front of a porch-buckled house clutched in a fist of kudzu. A dead fern sits on the front step, its fronds ossified into the shape of human vertebrae.

Sarah's father leaps from the truck and roots around under the blue tarp, resurfacing with a gigantic turkey he hugs to his chest like a baby. Sarah watches as he navigates the decayed porch while balancing the turkey. Eventually, the front door opens, and a skinny, blond dude in his boxers emerges, his hand visored over his eyes against the new sun. His shoulders snap together when he recognizes his boss. The man seems to know the sweet spot on the porch; he moves across one board toward her father with a strangely delicate grace. There's a lot of awkward smiling and nodding as her father rolls the turkey into the guy's cupped arms, a slap on the man's naked bicep as they part, and then her father is back in the truck, keying the next address into the GPS.

They hit several more houses in town, most of them in a similar state of disrepair. Her father took her phone for the day, so Sarah fiddles with the radio as she waits in the truck, making it a point not to watch the gifting of the turkeys. Then they head out toward Highway 280, past the high school and the Family Dollar and the local psychic's house with the man-sized sign of a poorly painted palm print stuck to the front that, if Sarah squints her eyes just right, looks as if something like God is reaching through the brick to offer her an enthusiastic high five.

They pass the Hardee's, where a bent old man with an industrial-sized broom sweeps the parking lot, a futile endeavor if ever there was one. With the students loosed for Thanksgiving, the parking lot—the jock and cheerleader hangout—will fill by dusk with kids escaping their families, the boys sitting on their tailgates talking shit about each other's trucks, the sloe-eyed girls chain-smoking and thumbing the screens of their phones while they wait for the boys to notice them, their lazy exhalations edged with a palpable anger.

Sometimes Sean allowed Sarah to tag along with him on Friday nights after his games. They would eat mountains of french fries and watch the spectacle of high school play out before them. Sean, just starting his junior year, had a drawer full of letters from smaller colleges around the Southeast, and, still juiced from the game, he'd talk excitedly about how things were going to be different for him, how no fucking way would he end up like the few other local boys who'd played college ball, coming home after graduating or flunking out and cruising the town in their tricked-out trucks hunting high school pussy.

Eventually, whichever remarkably uncheerful cheerleader Sean was hooking up with at the time would knock on Sean's window, pissed at being ignored, and Sarah would find herself displaced by the girl, waiting in the fluorescent-lit restaurant alone, watching through the window while Sean and the girl fought inside the truck, then, Sean's bulk pressed against the girl, made out, which looked to Sarah like another kind of fighting.

"Almost done," Sarah's father says. His thighs piston against the seats with the beat of a tune about a girl digging a man for his tractor, which is about the stupidest thing Sarah has ever heard. Sarah hasn't seen him this energized in months, not since Sean's last game, when he'd paced in front of the bleachers with a rowdy posse of other dads, all of them drinking booze-spiked sodas and yelling obscenities at the other team, the coaches, the ref, and, sometimes, each other. This was before a three-hundred-pound linebacker from LaFayette planted his boulder-sized head into her brother's helmet on a quarterback sneak.

They drive out of town, a few miles up 280 toward Camp Hill, and turn off on a dirt road Sarah would have never noticed. It takes a good ten minutes, long enough that Sarah wonders if they might be lost, but eventually a pretty yellow cottage with a bright white porch appears in the middle of a pecan grove. A little black girl sits in a dented wading pool in the front yard, a throng of older boys tossing a ball over her head. A few trucks and cars are parked in front of a shed, and her father pulls up beside them and cuts the engine.

"I need to go to the bathroom," Sarah says, the Gatorade and a can of Beanie Weenies not sitting well on her soured stomach. She doesn't really want to go inside a stranger's house, but she doesn't have much of a choice. She gets out and waits on her dad to dig a turkey from the back. The boys, middle school age, keep tossing the football as if Sarah is not there. The little girl in the wading pool studies Sarah warily, calls out, "I'm Iris. Who are y'all?"

Sarah walks over and peers into the pool. It's filled with several inches of red dirt. The girl, who looks to be about four or so, has a naked blond Barbie in each hand. She drags their long hair across the dirt, etching a crude alphabet.

"We brought you a turkey," Sarah says.

"We already got a turkey," the girl says.

Sarah hears her father's name called, and she looks toward the house and sees a tall, bald, black man leaning into the porch railing, waving.

"Good morning, Mr. Oliver," the man yells. "Come grab yourself some coffee."

Sarah follows her father up a well-kept stone path to the porch. He stomps the dirt from his boots at the base of the porch steps, then stands there with the turkey, staring up at the man, who towers over them, his thick-veined forearms a tattooed jungle of birds and naked women.

"This is Uncle Charley," her father says jovially. "He's my right-hand man at work these days."

"Yes, sir, yes, sir," Uncle Charley says.

"I'd be up a creek without Uncle Charley."

"I sure appreciate you saying that, Mr. Oliver." Uncle Charley grins, a huge smile that splits his face in half, the gap between his front teeth large enough to show the red of his tongue. "I'm grateful for the work. Times is tough. Nobody else would even give me a chance. All I wanted was an honest day's work."

Sarah walks over and peers into the pool. It's filled with several inches of red dirt.

"That's all a man deserves."

Both of the men nod their heads solemnly.

Her father jerks his chin her way. "This is Sarah, my daughter. I'm taking her on her first hunt today."

"Oh, I don't believe that, not at all. I bet you done killed all kinds of young bucks already." Uncle Charley winks at Sarah, and she feels her cheeks burn.

Her father hefts the turkey a few inches. "We brought you a little something for tomorrow. Just a small thank-you for all your hard work."

"You're a good man, Mr. Oliver," Uncle Charley says. "A good man."

"It's the least I could do."

"You done plenty already, Mr. Oliver," Uncle Charley says. "Let me get y'all that coffee."

Uncle Charley leads them through the tidy living room to the kitchen, which smells of bacon and piecrust and strong coffee. A young man, a kid, really, as tall and wide as Uncle Charley, sits at the kitchen table drinking a glass of orange juice and reading a book. Sarah doesn't recognize the boy from school, but there is no reason she would aside from the sheer size of him. The students self-segregate at assembly and lunch, the black kids on one side of the auditorium or cafeteria, the white kids on the other, and the skanks and weirdoes of all colors—mostly fat kids and slow kids—in the no-man's-land in the middle. Sarah and her friends sit on the white side, precariously close to the middle.

"Mr. Oliver, this is my nephew, Will," Uncle Charley says. He hands them each a cup of coffee from the French press on the stove, and Sarah takes a sip, the taste so bitter she almost vomits on Uncle Charley's floor.

The young man glances up from under his glasses, eyes her father, then the turkey, then Sarah. He wears a shirt with MISSISSIPPI STATE written across the front in maroon block letters.

"Mr. Oliver manages us men at work," Uncle Charley says.

"So you're my uncle's boss man?" Will says.

"I don't sign the checks," her father says, laughing. "But I hand them out."

Will doesn't laugh back.

"Will's my sister's boy," Uncle Charley says quickly. "He's a sophomore up in Starkville."

"What do you study?" Sarah's father asks.

"Philosophy," Will answers.

> Her friends have a communal attitude toward coupling; usually, proximity is the deciding factor.

"He got himself a full ride," Uncle Charley says.

"I'm going to set this down here," Sarah's father says of the turkey, and he rolls it onto the kitchen table in front of Will. It wobbles like a top.

"You passing out the holiday rations?" Will asks.

Her father's face slackens. He stares at the boy as if he's missed something. "It's a turkey," he says. "A gift."

"It's never just a turkey," Will says.

Uncle Charley laughs too loudly. "You know these kids," he says. "They go off to school and come home full of piss and vinegar. Get all kinds of ideas."

"You play ball?" her father asks Will, trying, Sarah can tell, to make nice.

Will closes his book. There's a picture of a half-naked black man riding a horse painted like an American flag on the cover. "No," he says, enunciating slowly, "I don't play ball."

"My son played quarterback," Sarah's father says, looking like he might cry at any moment.

Sarah's stomach careens against her ribs. "You got a bathroom I can use?" she asks.

The bathroom is papered in pink and gold flowers. It smells of bleach and potpourri. Sarah sits on the toilet long enough she's embarrassed to leave. Stalling, she goes through the medicine cabinet, half hoping to score, but finds only baby aspirin and laxatives.

Sarah catches her reflection in the mirror and is startled, for a moment, by what she sees there. Her history teacher is always telling some horrific story of strife—students slaughtered in China, civil rights activists murdered in Mississippi—then asking the class dramatically, *Who will you choose to be in this world?* She examines herself, the dyed black hair, the nose ring, the wings of thick eyeliner arched up toward her brows. She knows she is staring at her own image, but it is as if she has borrowed some other girl's face. If she sticks her tongue out, there's a distinct possibility that the girl in the mirror will not do the same.

Her bottom lip is slightly bruised, a small cut puckering the fragile skin, and she thinks of her friend Andy, what he'd said last night. "All evidence of the truth, sweet Sarah, comes only from the senses." He said it as he fingered her against the door of his mom's ancient Volvo wagon.

Sarah'd hooked up with Andy a few times at the cabin, a fish camp that belonged to somebody's grandfather who was too old or sick to use it anymore. Her friends have a communal attitude toward coupling; usually, proximity is the deciding factor, and Sarah ends up with whoever is slouched next to her when she's finally too stoned to have much of a preference. Even so, Andy, with his pretentious quotes, his pocked skin, and gauged, udder-like earlobes, mildly repulses her, though it takes more effort to tell him no than it does to wait out the manhandling.

"You mean my vagina is the key to the great truths of the universe?" Sarah had said, laughing, and she was mainly joking, but part of her wanted him to tell her that yes, something extraordinary and unknown lies dormant inside her, a wondrous mystery waiting to reveal itself.

He'd yanked his hand from under her skirt and slapped her across the mouth. "You feel that?" he asked before walking casually up the steps back to the cabin, where she could see shadows on the porch writhing to the music, a painful dirge that scudded across the lake like a thousand skipped rocks.

She presses her tongue to the cut now. The sting is not unpleasant.

When Sarah finally emerges from the bathroom, she makes her way to the kitchen, but no one is there. She finds Iris in the living room, watching cartoons on the couch. Will sits beside her, his book open in his lap, an index finger tracing a line of text on a page. He does not bother to look up when Sarah clears her throat to signal her presence in the doorway. "Your daddy's waiting in his truck," the girl says, not taking her eyes off the cartoon. A long-lashed mouse is beating a cat over the head with a toaster.

Her father doesn't say anything when she gets into the cab. They are almost to Opelika when he pulls off at a gas station and stuffs the last two turkeys in the trash can by the pumps. He buys a pint of bourbon from the attached liquor store and takes a draw as soon as he slides back into the driver's seat. The jeep at the pump in front of them has a buck tied to the roof, and its luminous eyes fix on Sarah. It looks as if it might reanimate at any moment, leap off the jeep, and return to whatever it is that deer do.

"Maybe your mother's got the right idea." Her father takes another sip of bourbon, turns the radio on, then thinks better of it and turns it off. "Why bother?"

"What bad choice did he make?" Sarah asks. "Why wouldn't anybody hire Uncle Charley?"

"Nothing worse than anybody else," her father says.

When they get to his buddy's land, the access gate has not been unlocked as promised. Her father tries calling his friend, and when no one answers, he decides to scale the fence to see if it's doable for Sarah. He makes it halfway up before his boot gets caught in the wire and he falls hard, jamming his right hand. Within minutes, it swells to twice its size.

"It's okay," Sarah says. "I didn't really want to kill anything anyway. Hunting was your and Sean's thing."

"We're starting too late anyhow," he says. He stares at her for a long moment, then asks, "Why did you do that to your hair, Sarah? It looks like shit." There's something mean and sad in his voice, and Sarah understands that those two things can sometimes be one and the same.

"It's just hair," Sarah says. "I can change it back anytime." But her father shakes his head slowly from side to side, as if such a thing is an impossibility.

It's a nice day, the air crisp, the sky a ribbon of flawless blue, so they decide to eat their lunch on the tailgate before returning home. Her father made tuna fish sandwiches, a favorite of Sarah's, and she manages to get half of one down. He eats some potato chips, but mainly he drinks the bourbon with his left hand, his right plunged into the cooler.

The cars rush by in a lulling cadence. Sarah lies back on the bed of the truck, the piney woods swaying in the breeze. Sarah's mother once told her of a woman, a mother of a classmate, who'd gone missing years ago when Sarah's mother was in high school, how she and her friends had searched with the town for the body in woods not far from here, how they never located her, never knew if the woman had been killed or taken, or if maybe she'd just left. Sarah and her friends would sometimes play hunt-the-body in the woods behind Sarah's house, taking turns as the dead woman, lying stone-still under some brush or in a natural depression in the earth, waiting to be found. Sarah's mother had shared the story, Sarah knew even then, as a subtle threat not to take her for granted, a warning that she could be gone in one way or another in the blink of an eye.

"You think Mom will cook anything tomorrow?" Sarah asks. She sits up, the world spinning before it steadies itself.

"No," her father says. "I don't." He shoves the bag of potato chips into the cooler. "We best be going."

The jeep at the pump in front of them has a buck tied to the roof, and its luminous eyes fix on Sarah.

Sarah packs up what's left of the lunch and slides the cooler into the cab. When she moves to climb into the passenger seat, he tosses her his keys. "You drive," he says. "It'll be good practice."

Sarah's a few months shy of sixteen, but Sean let her drive his truck sometimes, and for weeks she's been taking her mother's car on short joy rides when her father's at work. She settles behind the steering wheel, arranging the seat and mirrors like she was taught in driver's ed.

Her father, impatient, pushes the gear in drive. "The best way to learn to drive," he says, "is to drive."

Sarah buckles up and inches onto the road, taking it slow for the first mile or two, but the truck, an automatic, doesn't drive all that differently than her mom's Camry, and once she gets used to its mass, she begins to enjoy sitting so high up off the ground, the powerful surge of the larger engine when she pumps the gas.

"Now we're cooking." Her father rests his head against the passenger side window. "I was just trying to think about something else, somebody else, anything else," he says. "I wanted to do something that made me feel good."

A minivan roars up on their tail, then passes on a solid line. Sarah can see child car seats in back. "Idiots," she says, feeling very grown up.

"Why'd that kid have to be such an asshole? Just take the damn turkey for Christ's sake."

The deer slams into front of the truck out of nowhere, its face pressing into the windshield with the suddenness of a ghoul in a horror film. Its black lips twist against the glass. Blood bubbles from its mouth like someone is blowing in it with a straw. Sarah loosens her grip on the steering wheel for just a second, and they veer into the oncoming lane before her father grabs the wheel and yanks them back.

Sarah is shaking, her entire body vibrating, her knees banging the underside of the steering column. She manages to ease onto the shoulder, the deer still riding the hood. They sit for a moment looking at the deer looking at them. Its breath webs the windshield. It makes an awful squealing sound.

> **The deer, a small four-point buck, is dead by the time they try to remove it from the hood.**

"You got to be fucking kidding me," her father says. He opens his door and stumbles out, unsteady on his feet. "C'mon, Sarah, with this lame hand I'm going to need some help."

Mercifully, the deer, a small four-point buck, is dead by the time they try to remove it from the hood. Her father grabs one hind leg and Sarah grabs the other, and on his count, they tug. It thunks to the ground, fur and flesh still stuck in the windshield wipers and grill. Big chunks of hide are missing from one side, but it doesn't look that bad, considering.

"What are we going to do with him now?" Sarah says.

At her father's instruction, Sarah parks in the same spot from earlier that day. The young boys are still throwing the football. Iris digs in the wading pool again, a cloud of red dirt rising around her. Sarah can see Uncle Charley and Will standing on the front porch. A few women sit near them in rocking chairs, large bowls wedged between their feet, ears of corn in their laps.

Her father hops out of the truck and Sarah follows, uncertain as to what is happening. Blood and fur pepper her shirt and jeans. It took them the better part of a half hour to maneuver the dead buck into the bed of the truck, her father cussing a streak through most of it, but he seems almost jubilant now. He pops the tailgate, then waves wildly at the porch with his good hand.

"Mr. Oliver," Uncle Charley calls. "Everything all right?"

"We're good, we're good," her father hollers back. "Just thought you and your nephew might could help me out here."

There's some rumbling on the porch, and it looks like Uncle Charley is saying something to Will that Will does not want to hear. The women keep rocking and shucking, unperturbed by the men. Eventually, Uncle Charley steps off the porch and walks toward their truck, Will following at a reluctant pace behind him.

"Oh," Uncle Charley says when he sees the deer. "You got yourself a good eater."

"We came by it the hard way," her father says. He points to the front of his truck. The grill is bent in half. Then he lifts his hurt hand, which doesn't look much like a hand anymore.

"Ouch," Uncle Charley says. "You need some ice for that?"

Sarah's father taps the pint of bourbon in the breast pocket of his shirt, says, "I took my medicine."

Will stops a few feet away, kicks at the ground with his sneakers. His left eye is bloodied and sealed shut, his pulpy top lip twice the size of his bottom.

Her father's eyes flicker from Will's face to Uncle Charley's, where he meets and holds Uncle Charley's unblinking gaze.

"Looks like you could use a drink, too," her father says, extending the bourbon toward the boy.

"No thank you," Will says faintly.

"With my hand busted, I ain't worth much." Her father gestures toward the deer. "I thought y'all might be willing to help me dress out this bad boy."

"I've never dressed a deer," Will says. His good eye widens with alarm. "I don't even know what that means."

Uncle Charley stands next to Sarah's father. He's a least a foot taller, his biceps the same diameter as her father's neck. His fists, the knuckles a raw red, tighten for just a second, and then he smiles his gapped smile. "We'd be happy to, Mr. Oliver."

"Excellent!" her father says. "Where's your skinning hoist?"

Uncle Charley points to an oak at the right of the shed; what looks like a hanger with hooks on the bottom corners dangles from a rope strung over a branch. Her father jumps into the truck and backs it up to the oak's trunk, then Uncle Charley and her father, who isn't much help, work the buck toward the tailgate. When the deer's sprawled half out of the bed, Uncle Charley pulls a fold-out knife from his jean's pocket and gouges a hole in the big joint of each hind leg. He finally gets the buck's legs, slippery with blood, lodged on the hooks. The younger boys have crowded around the carcass, and they poke it with sticks, giggling and shoving each other.

Uncle Charley strains as he winches the deer off the bed of the struck, but eventually the deer rises, its head and front hooves hanging limply toward the ground, and Sarah doesn't want to, but she can't help but think of her brother after the accident, of the long days he spent lying unmoving in the hospital bed, half his head shaved where they'd drilled the hole into his skull. Before they took him off life support, the doctors explained everything to her family, how Sean was no longer Sean, his brain a jumbled network of highways to nowhere, a miscarriage of neurons. But there was still something inside her brother—that miraculous and terrifying and unnameable thing. Sarah sensed it when she held his hand before they turned off the machines, and then later, when she kissed his cheek before they took his body, it was gone.

"I think he's up there good," Uncle Charley says, stepping back to admire his handiwork. "Let me get my skinning knife from the shed."

"I got mine," Sarah's father says. He fishes in his toolbox and finds a long, leather-handled knife. Uncle Charley reaches for it, and her father says, "I thought I'd let Will here give it a try."

Will looks petrified. He stares at the knife as if he's never seen one. "I told you," he says, "I don't know anything about cutting up a deer."

"This'll be your first lesson, then," her father says. There's a firm resolve in his voice. His expression beneath the bill of his hat almost reverent. "Every man should know how to dress a deer."

"Sure enough," Uncle Charley says. He tugs the boy toward the buck, then points at the pelvis, tells him to start below there and move toward the ribs, using only the tip of the blade so as not to rupture the gut sack and spoil the meat.

The deer—its legs spread wide, its genitals a tender swelling, exposed— looks indecent to Sarah, a terrible violation.

Will takes the knife and places its point hesitantly against the lower abdomen. His shoulders shake, but it is hard to tell if he is crying. He jabs the blade, then yanks his hand away. The knife stays put, like a dart stuck in a board.

"You can't hurt it," Uncle Charley says. "It's already dead. Just gut the damn thing."

Will takes a deep breath and grips the knife handle with both hands. He braces himself, turning his head away from the deer's belly, as if he can't bear to release what's inside.

"Go on, son," Sarah's father says, not unkindly. "We all had to learn somehow." 🛡

CONTRIBUTORS

Jodi Angel's second collection of stories was *You Only Get Letters from Jail*. She lives in Northern California with her wife and daughters.

Catherine Barnett is the author of *The Game of Boxes*, which won the 2012 James Laughlin Award, and *Into Perfect Spheres Such Holes Are Pierced*.

Mary Barnett is a choreographer, a mother of three, and a student at Yale Divinity School.

Cody Carvel grew up in Oklahoma and Texas. He has degrees in English and African-American Studies from Harvard and an MFA from USF.

Diana M. Chien's poetry has appeared in the *American Reader* and won awards from the *Atlantic* and others. She is a PhD candidate in microbiology at MIT.

Jonathan Russell Clark is a literary critic and fiction writer. His work has appeared in the *Georgia Review*, the *Millions*, the *Rumpus*, and elsewhere.

Jennifer S. Davis is the author of two collections of short stories, *Her Kind of Want* and *Our Former Lives in Art*. She teaches at LSU.

Edward Gauvin's translations have been honored by PEN America, the NEA, and the Lannan Foundation. His work includes over 200 graphic novels and sixty short stories.

Rita Gabis's *A Guest at the Shooters' Banquet: My Grandfather and the SS, My Jewish Family, A Search for the Truth* is forthcoming this fall.

David Gessner is the author of nine books, including the brand-new *All the Wild that Remains: Edward Abbey, Wallace Stegner, and the American West*.

Robert Duncan Gray is an English artist currently living and working in Portland, Oregon. He is the curator and host of À reading series.

Jessica Handler is the author of *Braving the Fire: A Guide to Writing About Grief and Loss* and *Invisible Sisters: A Memoir*.

Kimiko Hahn is the author of nine collections of poetry. She teaches in the MFA program in Creative Writing & Literary Translation at Queens College, CUNY.

Smith Henderson's first novel, *Fourth of July Creek*, won the 2014 Montana Book Award. He was a 2011 PEN Emerging Writer.

Greg Hrbek's new novel, *Not on Fire, but Burning*, will be published in fall 2015.

Lewis Hyde is at work on a new book, *A Primer for Forgetting*. He teaches at Kenyon College in the fall; the rest of the year he lives in Cambridge, Massachusetts.

Tara Ison is the author of the recent *Reeling Through Life: How I Learned to Live, Love, and Die at the Movies* and the forthcoming story collection *Ball*.

Paul Kirchner is a writer and illustrator living in Connecticut. A collection of his earlier bus strips is available on Amazon.

Patrick Modiano won the Nobel Prize for Literature in 2014.

John Reed is the author of *A Still Small Voice*, *The Whole*, *Snowball's Chance*, *All the World's a Grave*, and *Tales of Woe*. JohnReed.org

Rachel Riederer is an editor at *Guernica: a magazine of art & politics* and teaches at the City University of New York.

S. Shankar's most recent novel is *No End to the Journey* and his most recent critical book *Flesh and Fish Blood*. He also translates from Tamil.

Ed Skoog is the author of two books of poems, *Rough Day* and *Mister Skylight*, both published by Copper Canyon Press.

Sarah Elaine Smith is the author of *I Live in a Hut*. Her stories and poems have appeared in FENCE, *Better*, *jubilat*, and more.

Matthew Socia received an MFA from Emerson College. He has been published in *CutBank* and *Epiphany*. Originally from northern Michigan, he now lives in Connecticut.

Jenny Xie has work appearing in the *Literary Review*, *LA Review of Books*, *Gulf Coast*, and elsewhere. She teaches writing at NYU.

CREDITS:

"Forgetting Mississippi" is adapted from *A Primer for Forgetting* by Lewis Hyde forthcoming by Farrar, Straus and Giroux, LLC. Copyright © 2017 by Lewis Hyde. All rights reserved.
    FBI photographs of the skeletal remains courtesy of David Ridgen.
    David Ridgen's 2011 film, *Reconciliation in Mississippi*, is available online at www.vimeo.com/42827267.

FRONT COVER:

Nereid, Oil on Canvas, 18" x 24", 2014. © Shanon Playford. www.shanonplayford.com

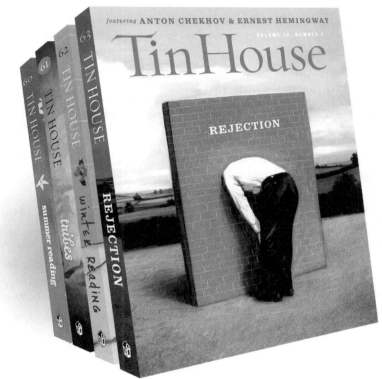

BookBrowse
Your Guide To Exceptional Books

Books you'll stay up all night reading, books that will whisk you to faraway places and times, books that will expand your mind and inspire you.

BookBrowse features the kinds of books you can't wait to talk about, providing insightful reviews, stories behind the books, excerpts and interviews. Our twice-monthly online magazine features all that's new; or you can browse by genre, time period, setting and theme to find the books that are just right for you.

In addition, we bring you readalike suggestions for thousands of books and authors; and previews of the top 80 books each month. Members can also request free books to read and review, or discuss.

- Reviews & "beyond the book" articles
- Excerpts, interviews & biographies
- Fiction & nonfiction
- Professional reviewers
- Browse by genre, setting, time period and theme
- Read-alike suggestions by book and author
- Reading guides & book club advice
- Book discussions
- Free books (US only)

We are people who love and have spent a lifetime with books. As a lawyer, author, lit major and publisher, I am astonished at the service you provide. I am always grateful for the depth and insight evident in your recommendations." ~Karen

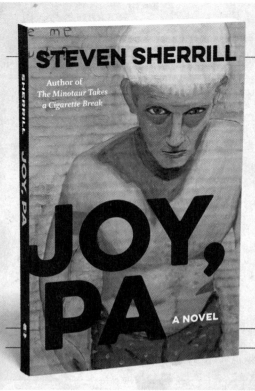

CaLARTS MFA CREATIVE WRITING PROGRAM

» A unique non-tracking curriculum

» Critical context for creative work

» Unparalleled interdisciplinary opportunities

» A dedicated, award-winning faculty

» Close mentorship

» Active professional development

» Home to the Katie Jacobson Writer in Residence Program and the Truman Capote Fellowship

» Host of the &Now 2015 Literary Festival

RECENT AND UPCOMING VISITORS:

Lydia Davis
Edwidge Danticat
Samuel Delany
M. NourbeSe Philip

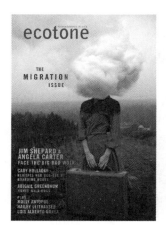

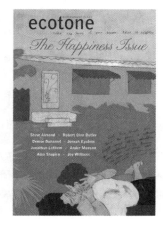

ABOUT THE COVER

The cover of our Summer Reading issue features Shanon Playford's *Nereid*, a painting from her *Oh My Gods!* series of classical figures depicted through modern imagery. In Greek mythology, the Nereids were the fifty daughters of Doris, a sea nymph, and Nereus, the Old Man of the Sea. They were also companions of Poseidon and patrons of sailors—guiding them through tumultuous seas to safe shores.

Playford positions her art within the Chameleon School of Painting, a fictional movement that encompasses her versatile style and the ways in which she adapts her methods to suit whichever theme she is currently exploring. Working in collections, Playford first selects a concept and then determines the best way to express it. She says that "with every new series, there is usually a new challenge" in the form of a previously untouched subject, style, or medium.

Lately, Playford also aligns with a kind of Poetic Realism. That is, she's "not interested in painting just what's before [her], but something more elusive." She achieves this in a seamless fusion of contemporary aesthetics with "close associations to the rich history of painting." This richness is nourished through research and a wide range of influences. A self-professed "Vermeer geek," her inspirations span art history, from the Dutch masters to the etchings of Goya to the para-realism of Lucian Freud.

Playford, a sixth-generation Portlander, is currently working on a series of one hundred views of Oregon. You can see more of her art at www.shanonplayford.com.

Written by *Tin House* designer Jakob Vala, based on an interview with the artist.